Tales from Victoria Park

Tales from Victoria Park

Todd Crowell

BLACKSMITH BOOKS

Tales from Victoria Park
ISBN 978-988-16139-3-6

Published by Blacksmith Books
Unit 26, 19/F, Block B, Wah Lok Industrial Centre,
37-41 Shan Mei Street, Fo Tan, Hong Kong
Tel: (+852) 2877 7899 • *www.blacksmithbooks.com*

Edited by Grahame Collins
First printing 2015

Also by Todd Crowell:
• *Dictionary of the Asian Language*
• *Explore Macau: A walking guide and history*
• *Farewell, My Colony: Last Years in the Life of British Hong Kong*
• *Tokyo: City on the Edge*

Supported by

香港藝術發展局
Hong Kong Arts Development Council

Contents

I.

END OF RAMADAN

Leila emerged from the subway exit and walked toward Victoria Park. It was *Idul Fetri*, the end of Ramadan, and the street was already crowded with Indonesian women, many of them having just returned from sunrise services marking the end of the fasting month. They had been held on the cricket field at the old Indian Club, since there were not enough mosques to hold the thousands of Muslim women now living in Hong Kong. Leila joined the crowd of women walking toward the park, talking and laughing among themselves, holding hands and looking forward to a carefree holiday, far from the apartments where they washed the clothes, made the meals, and cared for the children of thousands of Chinese and foreign families in the city. Many were wearing brightly-colored headscarves, creating a festive palette of colors: mauve, bright blue, pale green, pink and yellow.

But not Leila. Although she had faithfully observed the fasting rules for the previous four weeks, she wore instead the new jeans that Ahmed had given her the week before to celebrate the coming of the end of Ramadan. This was the first time she was wearing them, and, combined with her nicest pale-blue sweater and boots, they made her feel very smart. She planned to meet Ahmed later. He lived a long way from the park, and his job as a doorman for a luxury hotel often kept him at work until very late. So they usually met in Victoria Park around noon and spent part of the afternoon making love in one of the many small love hotels nearby. As, for many domestic helpers in Hong Kong, her employer imposed a curfew in the evenings, so they could only spend a few hours together. The past month had been especially difficult since they both observed the rules of abstinence, which meant not only fasting but also no lovemaking during daylight hours. Today, she planned to end their fast.

She entered the park, looking for her cousin, but it was difficult to find any one person in the teeming crowd. In one cluster Leila spotted her friend Wiji and walked over to talk with her. Wiji, in her twenties and pretty, was wearing a smart new dress, which Leila eyed with appreciation. "A present from your boyfriend, *mbak*?" she asked.

"Yes," Wiji answered proudly. "It took me a while to convince him that it is the custom to buy new clothes for Eid. He had never heard of it."

"I suppose you'll insist on another present from him at Christmas," Leila said.

"Of course," said Wiji. They both giggled. Then Wiji asked, "You're seeing Ahmed later?"

"Yes," Leila said. "He should be here by noon. I wish he could get here earlier." She looked at her watch. It was only about 9 a.m. She still had a long morning ahead of her.

"I'm going to meet Stephen later. He's still sleeping," said Wiji.

While Wiji chattered on, Leila let her eyes survey the park – the largest expanse of open space on crowded Hong Kong Island. Though early, it was already teeming with people. They lined the main pathways as far away as the model-boat pool. Already every one of the park benches was occupied. Where, on weekdays, elderly Chinese women and men lined up for their morning *tai-chi* exercises on the grassy infield, clusters of Indonesian women were staking out their territory for the day, laying down plastic sheets to sit on and spreading their lunch boxes and handbags to form little circles. It looked like an army bivouacked in an open field. Their voices were already rising and joining together in a steady hum, which made the park sound like one big aviary. And everywhere, the pungent smell of clove cigarettes. Hawkers were staking out their territory, spreading their wares in front of them, magazines, clothes, phonecards, music cassettes, and various kinds of Indonesian food.

Leila suddenly remembered that she needed to buy a phonecard so she could call her mother and wish her a happy Indonesian New Year. She nodded goodbye to Wiji and walked down the pathway to where several women had already established a kind of street market. She spotted Dina at her prime spot at the crossroads of several paths, sitting on a curb in

front of a large banyan tree. Magazines were spread out in front
of her on the pavement: *Tempo, Femina, Kosmopolitan*.

"*Majalah, kartu telpon*," she chanted to the women who
passed by.

"Hi Dina, can I have a phonecard?" Leila said.

Dina dug into her capacious handbag and brought out a
stack of cards, held together by a rubber band. She extracted
one and handed it to Leila. Then she took the proffered one-
hundred-dollar bill, reached into her handbag and handed back
a twenty. Leila noted that the handbag was already stuffed with
red and green Hong Kong-dollar notes, not to mention thick
wads of Indonesian rupiah.

"How's business?" She had decided to linger a while and
make conversation. The day was still early.

"Business is – " Dina's reply was cut off by the insistent
beeping of her mobile phone. She spoke a few words into the
mouthpiece, peeled off another phonecard and recited the
numbers. Then she wrote down the name of the buyer in a
small notebook.

"Good," she replied, snapping the telephone shut.

"So I can see," said Leila. She buried her own card in her
purse. She would call home in the evening, after curfew.

"Are you going to see Ahmed later, or does he have to work
today?" Dina inquired.

"No, I'm meeting him a little later here in the park." She
looked at her watch.

"I hear that every love hotel from North Point to Wanchai is already booked up," Dina continued.

Leila was a little surprised by Dina's sudden revelation. In fact, a couple hours in a hotel with Ahmed had figured prominently in her plans for this Sunday. But before she could reply, Dina's phone was beeping again.

Leila spotted Ahmed crossing the intersection to enter the park. She had been standing for two hours under the highway overpass, chatting with some of the other women, and she was anxious to see him. Ahmed gave her a chaste kiss on the cheek, and Leila introduced him to a couple of the women standing next to her. They looked at him appraisingly. He was a Pakistani, of medium height – though nearly a foot taller than Leila – and strongly built. He wore his customary outfit – a dark brown leather jacket and jeans. He looked around the park entrance – choked with women. "I haven't seen it so crowded. Let's go someplace else."

"Dina says every love hotel in Hong Kong is booked up."

Ahmed looked at her for a moment, confused.

"Dina?"

"You know who she is. The woman who sells magazines and changes money. She's here every day. Everybody knows Dina," Leila said.

"Oh," Ahmed replied uncertainly. In truth, he didn't spend that much time in Victoria Park. "How does she know? Come on, let's go."

They crossed the street, jostling with the crowds of Indonesian women who spilled out from the park, and hordes of Chinese Sunday-shoppers. In front of the Sogo department store they crossed Hennessy Road, then hiked up the street behind the Mitsukoshi department store to a part of Causeway Bay crowded with cheap hotels that rented rooms by the hour. They found a familiar doorway under a sign in English letters: "Venus Hotel." They entered the narrow elevator and rode it to the fourth floor, where it opened onto a reception area. They were surprised to see three couples sitting on the sofas. All tried to avoid eye contact. "No room, now. You wait," the old Chinese woman said.

Ahmed surveyed the room and calculated the waiting time. After all, there were only half a dozen rooms in the hotel.

"Maybe Dina was right," Leila said.

"Let's go and find someplace else," Ahmed replied.

They looked at three other hotels in the same neighborhood, but all of them were as crowded as the Venus Hotel. Not knowing what else to do, they walked aimlessly through the large shopping mall nearby. "I have an idea. Let's go back to Victoria Park and talk to Dina," said Leila.

"How can she help?"

"She has her own place close to the park. Perhaps she could let us use it for a couple of hours. She's busy today."

"You're the third couple that has asked me," Dina said cheerfully, when Leila and Ahmed found their way back to her spot. The spread of magazines in front of her had diminished considerably.

"I can't let you use it now, *mbak*. I have to go home soon and cut hair . . . "

". . . one couple offered me five hundred," she shouted as Leila and Ahmed walked away from her.

"Majalah, kartu telpon . . ."

It was already getting late in the afternoon. Leila suggested that they go to a disco, since it didn't look like they could find a room. Ahmed vaguely nodded agreement, and the two left the park once more and walked to the subway for the short ride to Wanchai. They could hear the steady thump of the disco music even as they emerged from the subway exit fifteen minutes later. The noise level increased to thunderous proportions as Ahmed pushed through the swinging door and started up the steep staircase, brushing past a couple of Filipina girls passing the opposite way. Ahmed paid the cover charge and they pushed through the rope curtain into the disco.

Ahmed and Leila stood still a few moments near the door while their eyes adjusted to the darkness. A small dance floor in front of them was jammed with women undulating together to the beat of a Filipino band. Strobe lights flickered from a round glass globe suspended from the ceiling. To the far end was the bar. Most of the bar stools were occupied by Western men, leaning forward and shouting into the ears of their young companions, or just nursing a drink and staring at the incredible writhing mass of femininity on the dance floor.

Ahmed left Leila standing at the edge of the floor and pushed his way toward the bar, like a schooner, plowing through the waves of women. He returned balancing two glasses of orange juice, trying to avoid bumping into the dancers. He handed one to Leila and looked around. Two women got up and left the disco, leaving a vacant place on the sofa, and Ahmed nudged Leila in that direction. The two sat down together, Ahmed bumping the low-lying drinks table with his bulk.

They stared silently at the dance floor, ignoring their drinks. Neither made a move to get up. Then, two Indonesian women came over to the table. "Have you been here long?" Yuni shouted over the din. She looked over at Ahmed and added archly, "I thought the two of you might be somewhere else this afternoon." Leila said nothing, and Yuni tossed her handbag in her direction. "Can you watch this?" she shouted. Before Leila could say anything, Yuni and her friend had moved to the edge of the dance floor and begun to dance together.

A few minutes later three other women entered the disco, brushing through the rope curtain, causing the wooden beads to clack. Leila stiffened as she recognized Retno. She had been Ahmed's girlfriend until they broke up six months previously. Ahmed had told her that he no longer went with Retno, but Leila wasn't so sure. She was trapped in her employer's apartment six days a week, while Ahmed was free to roam. Her eyes followed Retno and her companions as they moved deeper into the disco and disappeared into the gyrating crowd. She glanced over at Ahmed, but he was still staring straight ahead, seemingly unaware of their presence. But a moment later he heaved himself up from the sofa, again bumping his legs against the low-lying table.

"Toilet," he mouthed, as he moved in the direction of the bar.

Leila waited impatiently for Ahmed to return. As the minutes passed, she became increasingly anxious. She stared deeply into the disco trying to penetrate the mass of bodies to catch a glimpse of Ahmed. Once she thought she saw Retno, but it was difficult to tell for sure because the flickering strobe lights weirdly distorted the shapes of peoples' faces. She imagined that she could see Ahmed and Retno in deep conversation somewhere in the disco, Ahmed buying her a drink, the two of them on the dance floor, the two of them in a dark corner embracing – Ahmed's hands squeezing Retno's bottom. Abruptly, Leila pushed herself off the sofa, spilling her orange juice. She took only a few steps forward before bumping into Ahmed, returning from the toilet.

"What were you doing with her?" she blurted, pounding her fists against his chest. A few women standing nearby looked at them to see what was going on.

"Who? What?" Ahmed stammered.

"You can stay here with your girlfriend. I'm leaving," Leila shouted, and before Ahmed could respond, she turned, grabbed her handbag and stomped down the stairs.

"Leila!" said Ahmed, moving after her.

She walked briskly along Lockhart Road, her arms crossed. Ahmed caught up with her and walked by her side. They continued silently, block after block, back toward Victoria Park. It was already dark as they entered Causeway Bay. They began to run into streams of Indonesian women hurrying in the opposite direction, back to the subway entrances and the bus stops – back to their cramped servant quarters or boarding houses. In a few more hours the grounds would be deserted, save for clusters of old Chinese men playing checkers by the floodlights. Leila and Ahmed slumped down on one of the newly vacant park benches, breathing heavily from their long trek. For a few moments they said nothing. Then Ahmed spread one arm along the bench touching her shoulder, and Leila snuggled close to him. The exercise seemed to have dissipated Leila's anger. And as she rested, much of the fatigue also drained away, only to be replaced by a different sensation.

"You know I haven't had anything to eat all day," she told Ahmed.

"Neither have I." They both laughed at the irony of it.

"No food, no sex. I guess Ramadan isn't over for us," he said.

Leila looked at her watch. "I still have a little time left. Let's at least find something to eat." Ahmed nodded agreement, and

they both rose from the bench and walked hand-in-hand out
of the park.

2.

WIJI

One million, two million, three million. Dina counted the rupiah, collected the notes in an envelope, and stuffed them at the bottom of her purse. She took out a receipt booklet and carefully wrote down the amount: "Received from Wiji Astuti 10 million rupiah," and handed the piece of paper to the woman sitting next to her on the park bench.

"So this is the last payment on your rice field, *mbak*?" She closed her handbag and looked directly at the younger woman. Wiji was 25 and very attractive. Her long black hair fell halfway down her shoulders. Her wide lips were painted dark red. She was not tall, but she had a full figure. The men who prowled the park – mostly Chinese or Pakistani – stared at her, and sometimes made rude remarks.

"My brother said he will handle the deal, but Ihave to return to Indonesia to sign the papers myself. He said he cannot do it by himself."

"So when are you going home?" Dina inquired.

"I don't know for sure," Wiji replied, looking a little troubled. "You see, I've got a problem."

Wiji had worked as a maid in Hong Kong for four years. Her employer paid her a fair wage and gave her a considerable amount of freedom. She managed to save a large portion of her monthly salary – that part, anyway, that she did not spend on designer jeans and platform shoes. Even so, it would have taken considerably more than she could expect to save, to accumulate the 80 million rupiah she needed to buy the hectare of rice land in her home village in central Java.

Her family – three brothers and two sisters – had been surprised and proud when they first learned that their sister had, in only four years, earned enough money from working in Hong Kong to become a landowner. No one in her family had ever seen more than one or two million rupiah at any one time. "Our sister is doing very well in Hong Kong," they said to each other.

What Wiji was really doing in Hong Kong was having a good time. In her first year, she spent most of her free time sitting and gossiping with the other off-duty maids in Victoria Park. In the evening she often went back to her home, even though – unlike many of the other women – she had no curfew. Indeed, she could go out any evening, after she had finished fixing dinner and washing the dishes. Fairly soon she was dancing past midnight in the discos of Wanchai and began to acquire all the attributes of a pretty, single Indonesian woman in Hong Kong:

a mobile phone, an e-mail address, and a boyfriend – well, in fact, two boyfriends.

Stephen was a Canadian. His company sold kitchenware in China, and his business often took him to Hong Kong. In the evening he frequented the Makati Disco, where expatriate men came to pick up Filipina and Indonesian girls. Stephen was captivated watching Wiji undulating to the steady beat of the disco music. He soon gave up trying to pick up any of the other women and concentrated his attentions totally on Wiji. When he was away from Hong Kong he communicated with her almost daily, sending ardent e-mails to the account that he had set up for her. Wiji spent a couple hours on her day off reading through them at the internet cafe. When Stephen was in Hong Kong, she would slip out of her home after the evening meal and join him at the hotel where he regularly stayed, slipping out early to catch a taxi home before the rest of her employer's family awoke.

One night while lying in bed in Stephen's hotel room, in a languid mood after making love, Wiji started talking about her life growing up in a small town near Surakarta. She told him about walking barefoot past the rice fields to her school, about her parents' home and the chickens underfoot in the kitchen, about swimming in the nearby river. Almost in passing she mentioned that her mother had written that one of the neighbors was interested in selling some land. "It would be nice to be a landowner."

"How much would it cost to buy the land?" said Stephen, as he hauled himself out of the bed and walked over to the window, opening the curtains to view the skyline unfolding in the early morning light.

"I don't know. Maybe forty million rupiah."

"What's that in Hong Kong dollars?"

Wiji told him.

In fact, Wiji had no idea how much the land would cost, except that it would surely be more than she ever dreamed of possessing. The figure forty million was almost as high as she could imagine, and she was surprised when Stephen turned away from the window, walked back to the bed, kissed her gently on the forehead and said, "I'd like to help you buy the land."

"What did you do then?" asked Dina.

"I wrote my mother, and she wrote back saying that there was a farmer who wanted to sell a hectare of his land and he was asking ninety million for it. But my mother thinks he may come down to eighty million."

"So where are you going to get the other forty million?"

The other forty million came from Raymond. He was a Hong Kong Chinese she had met in Victoria Park. He was, like Wiji's Canadian lover, in his mid-30s, and held a job with a trading company that required he travel extensively in China, where he often bought presents. This constant travel satisfied Wiji, since it made it easier to juggle her two boyfriends. When one was in town, the other was almost always away on a business trip. They often went to eat *gado gado* at one of the small Indonesian restaurants in the area, then stayed at Raymond's apartment nearby.

Getting Raymond to provide the other forty million had taken considerable wile, but Wiji had been up to it. First she gave him the same idyllic story about her childhood in Indonesia and how she had dreamed of owning her own rice land to help take care of her future. When that story failed to elicit the same response she got from Stephen, she tried a more direct approach and asked Raymond if he could loan her the money to buy the land. "That's really all I need, and I'll be a landowner. I'll pay you back one thousand dollars every month."

Raymond thought this over for a while, calculating the months it would take Wiji to pay him back – and perhaps, the probabilities that they would be together long enough to recover the loan. Then he thought too of the pleasures he had had with Wiji, and he said, "There's no need to pay me back. I'll give you the money for the land."

Then something happened that Wiji had not counted on. Soon after the money was safely in her bank account, both Stephen and Raymond announced that they wanted to go with her to Indonesia – so that they could see the rice land they had helped her purchase – for themselves. Steven had never been anywhere in Indonesia, save for one week's holiday in Bali. Now he was excited about the prospect of seeing the real country. "I can't wait to see your village and meet your mother and brothers – to see where you went to school." He was beginning to get carried away. "What clothes should I wear? What kind of present should I buy your mother? Should we fly to Jakarta or Surabaya?"

Raymond was equally smitten with the notion of going to Wiji's village, as her great benefactor. "I have two weeks vacation coming. We could go to your home and then visit the palace at Jogjakarta – maybe see Borobudur." He had bought a guidebook of Java and was leafing through it in front of Wiji. "Should we fly to Jakarta or Surabaya?"

Wiji had no intention of introducing Stephen, Raymond, or any other foreign boyfriend, to her mother or the rest of the family. The idea of taking a Western boyfriend, or a Chinese boyfriend, to her conservative Muslim village was out of the question. And, of course, she could not go with one of them and not take the other. How did she get in such a fix? In the past it had been so easy to manage the two boyfriends. For a moment Wiji considered abandoning buying the rice field, but it was only for a moment. The prospect of becoming a landowner was too good to simply give up. Somehow she had to discourage both of them from making the trip.

"You know, I'm worried about you coming to my village," she said to Raymond one day.

"What do you mean?"

"Well, you know that Chinese are not very popular in my part of Indonesia. I'm afraid that you might get caught in a race riot and get hurt."

"Do they happen frequently in your place?"

"Well, sometimes," she said.

"Oh, I don't think I'll have to worry, as long as I'm with you."

The next time they were together, Wiji brandished an old letter from her brother. "My brother says there was a anti-Chinese riot just a few kilometers from my place. Some gangs attacked three Chinese-owned grocery stores and set two of them on fire. One of the grocers was killed and a woman got raped, he said." She flourished the letter in his face. He stared at the Indonesian words without comprehension. In fact, no riot had occurred anywhere near Wiji's home, but it so happened that the Hong Kong newspapers and television stations had carried reports of disturbances near the Sumatran city of Medan. Raymond had only a vague idea where Medan was located. It could easily have been a few kilometers from Wiji's place. "I'll make sure that everybody knows that you helped me buy my land," Wiji promised, as she noted Raymond's determination to make the trip begin to falter.

Wiji was pondering how to discourage Stephen from going with her to Indonesia when the perfect excuse arose. The bloody bombing of a disco, popular with Western tourists, in Bali had made headlines everywhere. Later she went to the internet cafe and wrote a message to Stephen in Canada:

I am disappointing darling that you decide not to go to Indonesia with me but I understand. Hope you are not too disappointing to. Don't worry about me. I take care. So don't be upset, sweety.

Love XXXX
Wiji

A few weeks later, Wiji was back in Victoria Park, sitting on the bench next to Dina. From her handbag she pulled out a sheaf of color photographs and showed them to her.

"This is my mother," she said, pointing to a diminutive woman with a wrinkled, leathery face, half shrouded in a brown headscarf. She also pulled out pictures of her brother, her sister, her cousins, her cousin's baby. . . Then she produced another shot of a brown expanse of ground, churned over, with rice stubble still on it. "And this," she said proudly, "is my rice field."

"Are you going to show these pictures to Stephen and Raymond?" asked Dina.

"Oh, I have a special picture for each of them," she said, pulling another set of photos out of her handbag. On one of them was a picture of the rice land with a crude sign attached to a stick, and reading, in English:

This rice land
Purchased with

Generosity of

Mr. Stephen Martin

Then she pulled out another picture. It had the same crude sign, only it read:

This rice land

Purchased with

Generosity of

Mr. Raymond Wu

"I'm going to give this picture to each of them."

"Be careful that you don't mix them up," said Dina. Wiji giggled.

"You didn't tell your mother or brothers about how you got the money to buy the rice land did you?"

"Oh, no," said Wiji. "I told my family that I saved the money for the land from my job, and from some part-time work that I do on my holidays. They were very proud."

3.

Nurma's Place

The sign outside of the door still read "Marco Polo Cosmetics Co.," but everybody just called it "Nurma's Place." This warren of tiny rooms, in a nondescript apartment building, was a home-away-from-home for many of the Indonesian women working in Hong Kong. On Sundays, Nurma's Place looked like a sorority house. The women began arriving as early as 7 a.m., crowding the narrow elevator to ride to the third floor. They spent their days lounging on the big black leather sofa in the main sitting room, gossiping and laughing with their friends, and shoveling rice – that Nurma and her helper, Rita, provided steadily at all hours – into their mouths. Sometimes they watched Indonesian karaoke programs on Nurma's television.

Others sat in the computer room working on six personal computers, three on one side of the wall and three on the other side. Each station was equipped with a camcorder, so that the women could go online and chat with their husbands and boyfriends back in Indonesia, or, more often, with their Western boyfriends. Many had met American sailors – passing through

Hong Kong – in Wanchai. And they kept in touch through e-mails and online chat rooms. Nurma charged the women a small fee by the hour, and if one peeked into the room, one would often find six heads, shrouded in scarves, staring into the screens, well into the evening.

Nurma's station was in the kitchen, just off the main room. There, she tended a large wok – filled with rice and chicken – through most of the day. She kept the table well stocked with *nasi goreng*, fried bananas and sticky rice. The women spooned them down from banana leaves, helping themselves to soft drinks or bottled water from the large refrigerator.

She was a big woman, in her late 30s, with closely cropped black hair. While working in the kitchen, she often wore an old sarong and flip flops. Her only concession to fashion was jewelry. She loved gold, and wore eight gold rings – four on one hand, and four on the other – shining brightly against her dark skin. She often wore a gold cross around her neck, even though she was a Muslim.

She had never bothered to take down the "Marco Polo Cosmetics Co." sign outside her door. She didn't need to advertise her place – the women found their way there by word-of-mouth. And it helped to put off nosy neighbors, who might have alerted Immigration to the unusual numbers of Indonesian women who gathered there. Although there was nothing strictly illegal going on – Nurma promptly evicted any girl who used drugs – there were, of course, some who overstayed their visas. Only once had Immigration raided Nurma's Place. Two officers knocked on the front door and examined the identity cards of the women in the sitting room. Most of the girls had nothing to worry about, but the officers somehow overlooked two overstays who were hiding in the toilet.

The last customer did not usually depart until close to midnight, although there were always three or four women who slept over in the back bunk room, paying Nurma a daily fee. Most of them were maids – terminated from their jobs and waiting, hopefully, that their agents would find them a new employer before they had to return to Indonesia. Not a few of the women overstayed their visas – usually after being terminated by their employers and thrown out onto the street. The two weeks that Hong Kong allowed displaced maids to find a new employer passed quickly, and finding another employer in that short time was difficult, especially with the steady stream of replacements arriving constantly from Indonesia and the Philippines. Many of these displaced women hung around Nurma's Place for several weeks after the expiration of their visas, hounding their agents, and hoping that something would turn up.

Some of the more enterprising among them managed to line up part-time jobs. They either continued to stay at Nurma's Place, paying Nurma 500 dollars a month, or they moved out and set up their own places in boarding houses, usually with two or more other women. Some of them found boyfriends and moved out to live with them, or were set up in their own small apartments. A few worked nights in Wanchai, picking up Western men who frequented the discos there. But many others finally just gave up and turned themselves in. They were quickly and smoothly processed through the courts, given a suspended jail sentence, and deported back to Indonesia.

Then there was Lia.

Nurma tried to remember when Lia first came to her place, but it was impossible for her to keep straight the dozens of faces that passed through her establishment in any given month. And Lia didn't exactly stand out. She was a thin, shy waif of a woman, in her mid-20s. She didn't seem to have any friends. Her only possessions were a small carry-on suitcase that held all of her clothes and a battered guitar. Nurma thought she had been fired as a domestic helper, but she wasn't even sure about that. And she was too busy to inquire further.

One day in the middle of the week, when things were slow, Nurma, tiring of the closeness of her cluttered apartment, walked over to Victoria Park to get some fresh air. She found Dina sitting by herself in her usual spot. It was cold for Hong Kong, and Dina was bundled up in a green padded coat, her hands swathed in gloves. There were few other Indonesian women in the park.

Nurma and Dina had been friends for a long time. Both women were about the same age, and had moved to Hong Kong from Indonesia at a time, ten years previously, when there were far fewer Indonesian women living and working in Hong Kong. Dina used to cut Nurma's hair on Sundays in Victoria Park, while both of them were working during the week as maids. Later Dina visited Nurma's Place late in the afternoon when things got slow in the park, and she often ate fried rice there.

"How's business?" Nurma asked, as she settled down on the bench beside her.

"Not very many customers today. Too cold." Dina replied. "I had been thinking of going back to my place, but it is just as cold there. At least the sun is shining outside"

"You should come over to my place," said Nurma. "We have a heater." She paused. "Nobody's there except Rita," she said, referring to the middle-aged Indonesian woman who worked as her helper and did other chores … "and Lia, of course."

"Lia?" said Dina. "I don't remember anyone named Lia at your place."

"She's an overstay. She's been living at my place for . . . I don't remember how long. She eats my food and takes up a bunk but doesn't pay me anything. She never goes out, as far as I can tell. She just stays in the bunk room playing her guitar."

"Why don't you just turn her over to Immigration?"

"You know I can't do that," replied Nurma. There was a code among the Indonesian women in Hong Kong not to inform on each other. Too many of them had questionable legal status. Nurma herself had paid a Chinese man to marry her on paper so that she could become a permanent resident. "Anyway, I don't want to bring the attention of Immigration to my place. I've had some other overstays too, but at least they paid me."

"Sounds like she's found a home," said Dina. Nurma just gave her a side-long look and said nothing. They were silent for a few minutes. Dina hailed an Indonesian woman walking by the bench: "*majalis, kartu telphon, rupiah*," she chanted, waving a copy of *Tempo* at her, but the woman just walked by.

"I asked Rita to talk to her, but apparently she wasn't forceful enough, because she is still there and shows no sign of wanting to leave."

"Why don't you just throw her out? She can live on the street, like Retno."

Nurma thrust her hands deeper into her pockets. "I don't know. I don't see how I can force her out now, not in this weather. Even Retno is sleeping at Wati's place." Retno was another Indonesian overstay who often slept in the park on warmer nights, or spent the night sleeping in a booth in the dark, nether reaches of one of the Wanchai discos.

"Maybe she can find a boyfriend, who can take care of her, set her up in a small apartment," Dina suggested.

"How can she do that when she spends all of her time in my place and never goes out? Anyway, she's a kind of mousy looking woman. I'm not sure she could find anyone." Nurma tightened the button close to her neck. "I don't know how you can sit all day out in this cold," she said. "I think I'll go back to my place. Why don't you come too?" Dina looked at her watch – it was already getting late – gathered up her unsold magazines, and stuffed them into the small carry-on suitcase. "Let me just drop this stuff off at my place." Dina lived close to Victoria Park, just about a block away from Nurma's apartment building.

For the next few days, Nurma put Lia out of her mind. It was easy to do since Lia was so unassuming, and for the most part, stayed in the bunk room, only occasionally coming out to the main sitting room to watch karaoke on the television. She never used any of the computers, since she didn't have the money to pay for the time, and anyway, she apparently did not have anyone she wanted to chat online with. The weather stayed chilly for the next week. When it finally began to get warmer, Lia occasionally went out. Nurma didn't ask where she went, but Dina told her that she sometimes saw Lia walking alone in the park. But Lia did not go out very often, apparently because she was afraid that the police might stop and question her.

And Nurma had other things on her mind. She complained to Rita about the Indian man who worked as a watchman at the entrance to the building. It was impossible to avoid passing by him. He spent his day sitting in the little office next to the elevators, or lounging in a rickety wooden chair, eyeing everybody who came and went from the building. It seemed to Nurma that he paid special attention to her.

"I know," said Rita. "Sometimes he looks at me that way and makes some rude comments." Nurma smiled to herself. Rita was over 50, stout, and missing some of her teeth.

"Yes, but the other day he began to make some threats," said Nurma.

"What kind of threats?" Rita was suddenly alert.

"He said, 'I know what you are doing. Maybe I should tell the police that you are running a brothel'."

"What?" Rita was astonished. "How can he say that? No men come up here."

"I know," replied Nurma. "But I have the feeling that he is going ask for some money to keep quiet . . . or, maybe something else."

"Maybe you can interest him in Lia," Rita replied. Nurma looked at her, puzzled. She had almost forgotten about Lia . . . Lia, another problem.

"*Aaiiiyah!*," she exclaimed. "Maybe I should go back to Indonesia."

What she did was go to Macau. She left with Dina on a Monday – neither of them wanted to be away from Hong Kong on a Sunday, the busiest day of the week for both of them. The two women checked into the Presidente Hotel, where they spent most of the following two days in the hotel's casino. Nurma enjoyed playing blackjack, while Dina preferred the slot machines. When they were ready to return, Dina had lost nearly a thousand dollars, but Nurma was up by more than two thousand, so she felt in a pretty good mood.

She felt even better when, on returning to her apartment building, she noticed that the Indian watchman was gone, replaced by an old Chinese man who was nodding over his racing sheet. He ignored Nurma as she punched the button and waited for the elevator. Rita greeted her cheerfully when she entered the apartment. "How did things go?" Nurma opened her purse and pulled out four brown five-hundred-dollar notes and waved them in front of her. Rita snatched one of them from her hand. "That's to pay for the new modem I had to buy while you were gone."

Nurma walked into her bedroom and dropped her small satchel on the bed. Then she returned to the main sitting room. It was deserted. She wandered back into the computer room. One Indonesian woman was sitting in front of the console. She smiled briefly at Nurma and then returned her attention to the screen. She went further back into the bunk room. One of the newer girls was lounging on one of the beds, reading a magazine. Back in the sitting room, Rita told her about the little problems that had occurred while she was gone. "The water was off most of the day yesterday, fixing the main pipe . . . and, oh yes, Lia left."

"Lia?" Nurma looked over at Rita. "What do you mean she left? She went out?"

"No, I mean Lia left Monday, soon after you went to Macau. She took her stuff with her. She didn't come back last night or the night before. She didn't say where she was going."

Nurma walked back into the bunk room. She ignored the woman lying on the bed. To be sure, Lia's guitar was gone. So was Lia.

Nurma should have been happy to be rid of Lia, but for some reason she was worried.

"Do you think Immigration caught her?" she asked.

"Caught who?" Rita had already forgotten about Lia.

"Lia, of course," Nurma snapped. "But how come her guitar is missing?"

"I don't know. Maybe she pawned it."

Nurma turned the possibilities over in her mind. Lia might have moved in with another friend, except as far as Nurma could tell, she didn't have any friends. She might have found a new employer. But how could she do that, she wondered, if she didn't have a visa? She knew that some employers were not so particular if they knew they could get away with paying well below the minimum wage. But then, how could she have found a new job when she spent most of the day in her place? That left the possibility that she may have been caught by Immigration, or turned herself in.

The next morning Nurma boarded a bus for Central. She got off at Pedder St. and walked up Hollywood Road to Victoria Prison. The old goal, in the central part of Hong Kong lived up to its name, since it literally dated back to the Victorian era. These days it was utilized mainly as a holding station for overstays and other immigration cases, waiting to be deported back to their home countries. Nurma had been there before, and she knew the routine pretty well. She walked up Old Bailey St. to the visitor's entrance, rang the bell and was admitted by a security guard.

When she passed through the metal detector into the reception room she remembered that she didn't know Lia's full name. She wasn't even sure that Lia was her real name – so many Indonesian women in Hong Kong adopted different names – as if, by moving to Hong Kong, they had taken on a new identity. Nurma persisted, asking the female corrections officer – wearing a starched, drab, olive uniform – behind the desk if they had an Indonesian woman by the name of Lia. "I can't remember her last name."

"If you don't have her last name, I don't see how I can help," said the officer in crisp English. Nevertheless, she thumbed through her file. "There is nobody here named Lia, and no Indonesians were brought here in the last few days." Nurma thanked her and walked out. She returned to her place frustrated.

Early the next morning Dina was making her pre-dawn rounds in Wanchai. She often went there on Saturday mornings, to change money for the Indonesian women who worked the discos on Friday nights. Around the corner from the 7-Eleven store, where she usually sat on the stoop, she saw a woman throwing up against a wall. By itself, it wasn't such an unusual sight in Wanchai at this early hour. But something about her looked familiar, and she walked over to the retching woman.

"Lia?"

The woman just looked up at her and smiled wanly, not saying anything. Dina helped her to her feet, putting an arm around her shoulder. It was too early to catch a bus or a subway train back to Causeway Bay. So she placed Lia in a taxi and the two drove off, Lia slumped against her shoulder. In the short ride through the empty streets, Dina managed to get only a few words, but they were enough for Dina to put the picture together. Lia had gone to the disco to try to earn some money as a PR girl, sipping drinks with customers. From the looks of her, she didn't do it very well.

They stopped outside Nurma's building. Lia was alert enough to remember the door code, so they didn't have to wake the Chinese watchman who was slumped over his desk, sleeping. At the entrance to the Marco Polo Cosmetics Co., Dina pressed the buzzer until a sleepy Nurma cracked the door open. She opened it wider when she recognized Dina and her charge. She ushered the two women into the apartment and together they went to the toilet where they gently cleaned Lia's face.

A few days later Nurma dropped by Victoria Park and sat down beside Dina. "Where is Lia?" Dina inquired.

"Oh, she's still at my place. I got her guitar from the pawn shop with the little money she had earned at the disco."

"So you're going to let her stay?"

Nurma shrugged. "Rita is going home next month, and maybe Lia can help out around the kitchen." The two women looked at each other for a moment in silence. Then both of them broke out laughing.

4.

GOLDEN NEEDLES

Ani sat on a stool in front of a mirror in Dina's small apartment, which doubled as her hair salon. Dina wrapped a silk scarf around her shoulders and looked appraisingly at the woman's reflection in the mirror. "Where is Sumianti today, *mas?*" she asked her, using the word for "brother." Sumianti was Ani's lover, and constant companion, and they usually had their hair trimmed together. Indeed, they did everything together. "She's found someone else," Ani said tensely, frowning into the mirror. Dina was extremely surprised. For as long as she could remember Ani and Sumianti had been a couple. "Tell me about it," Dina said.

Ani had moved to Hong Kong five years previously. She worked as a maid for a Chinese family and slept in a small room in their modest apartment. She was 35 years old and had left behind a husband and two children, whom she had not seen since she had moved away from Indonesia. During the first couple years she was very lonely. On her day off she gravitated to Victoria Park, just to experience the company of other Indonesian women. Then, one Sunday, she met Sumianti.

She was sitting by herself on a park bench, wondering if she could go home, when Sumianti and two companions passed by and sat down on the vacant spaces. Listening to Sumianti talk to her friends, Ani thought she recognized a familiar accent, and she interrupted to ask where she was from. Sumianti turned her head towards the stranger and said, in a friendly way, that she came from Bawean island, off the northeast coast of Java – which was where Ani came from. Soon the two were chattering away in Baweanese, Sumianti having completely forgotten about her other companions.

Sumianti was younger than Ani – still in her late 20s – and single. She also had lived for about five years in Hong Kong, working for a British couple that lived in a large apartment in the Mid-Levels. She was outgoing, where Ani was shy, and popular with the women in the park. When Ani was with Sumianti, she felt popular herself. And Sumianti had a way of making a person feel important – full of questions about Ani's life back in Indonesia, her children and her husband. Pretty soon, Ani found herself thinking about Sumianti often during her working day, and she counted the days until Sunday when she could spend the whole day with her friend.

Soon Ani and Sumianti were inseparable. They spent their days off in each other's company, holding hands as they walked through Victoria Park, laughing and giggling and talking in their special dialect. Ani soon began to copy Sumianti's way of dressing, She wore baggy, mannish-looking trousers, a plain flannel shirt and heavy athletic shoes. She gave up wearing makeup, and had her hair cropped closely, like Sumianti. They began to look like twins and were accepted in the park as a couple.

Sometimes Ani visited Sumianti in the home of her employer, who had a large apartment on Robinson Road. Sumianti had her own room that opened off the kitchen and connected through the rear door, so they could come and go without disturbing the rest of the family. Ani never took Sumianti to her place, which was small and cramped by comparison. They could enter only through the front door – running the gauntlet of children and grandparents – to the tiny cubbyhole that Ani called home. Her bed, little more than a cot, was not big enough for both of them. Sometimes they preferred the comfort and anonymity of a cheap love hotel, lounging together on the large bed, holding hands and watching Chinese soap operas on the television screen suspended in front of them.

"Do you think we could live together like this back home?" Ani asked Sumianti one afternoon.

"What do you mean?" she replied.

"I'm serious," said Ani, turning over on her side and looking directly at Sumianti.

"What about your husband and children?"

"Oh, well, we could build a house next door, and I could visit them once a week," said Ani.

Both women burst out laughing.

But, of course, Ani did have a husband and children in Indonesia, and the time came when she could no longer put off taking leave from her job and making a trip home. Sumianti helped her shop for clothes and other presents to lug back with her, and helped her carry the bags to the airport on the afternoon that she left on a Cathay Pacific flight to Surabaya.

During the two weeks she spent in Indonesia, Ani's thoughts continually drifted back to Hong Kong, and Sumianti. Every other day, she left her house and walked down to the office of Indonesia Telekom, where she could make a long-distance phone call. At first, Sumianti seemed pleased to hear Ani's voice, and gossiped about her work and what was happening in the park. Towards the end of her holiday, however, the conversations got shorter, and once, Sumianti rebuked her for wasting so much money on long-distance phone calls. Her husband too, got a little suspicious about her trips into town. "Have you found somebody in Hong Kong?" he had asked. Just before she returned, she found that Sumianti's phone was turned off.

The holiday came to an end, and Ani entered the jetliner for the trip back to Hong Kong with an extra bounce in her step. She was not very concerned when she arrived and Sumianti was not at the airport to greet her. After all, it was in the late morning of a working day – difficult for any domestic helper to get free.

For several days, Ani tried to call Sumianti, but her telephone was always turned off. Finally, Sunday arrived, and she headed for Victoria Park. But Sumianti was not sitting on the park bench where she usually was found. Ani searched everywhere, on the "beach" fronting the yacht basin, near the model-boat pool, even around the tennis courts on the far side of the park, not usually frequented by Indonesian women. A few times she thought she spotted Sumianti's closely-cropped hair, but it turned out to be another woman.

One week later, Ani again headed toward the park, but this time the eager anticipation that she had felt the previous week was replaced with dread. By now she knew that something was not right. She half hoped that Sumianti had some misfortune at home and had gone back home to Indonesia. She even speculated that she had been terminated from her job and forced to leave Hong Kong.

Finally she spotted Retno standing in a crowd of other women under the highway overpass, and went over to question her.

"Have you seen Sumianti today, *mbak?*" she asked with studied casualness.

"Oh, don't you know? Sumianti has found herself another tomboy. They're always together." said Retno. Suddenly, it seemed to Ani as if she couldn't stand up. She might have buckled if she hadn't been leaning against the edge of the concrete support.

"Who . . . who is she seeing now?" Ani finally managed to stammer.

"I don't know. I think she is some young woman, just came here from Indonesia."

She tried calling Sumianti several times again on her mobile phone, but the phone just kept ringing and ringing. Sumianti could tell from her caller display who was calling, and obviously didn't want to answer. Ani's work began to suffer, and she seemed to spend hours lying on her cot in her tiny room staring at the ceiling. Several times her employer looked at her in a puzzled manner, and rebuked her for her lack of attention to her work. On her day off she prowled the park, trying to find Sumianti and see what her companion looked like.

Dina dropped the scissors to her side and studied Ani's face for a few moments. "You look pretty unhappy. Can't you find another friend?"

Then Ani burst into tears. "I don't know what to do. I'm so depressed."

"I know somebody who might be able to help you."

Several Indonesian women in Hong Kong claimed to be *dukuns,* native healers who had power to cast spells and tell fortunes. Some worked in Victoria Park on Sunday, answering simple questions, such as, "Is my boyfriend seeing another woman?" The woman that Dina recommended, however, worked out of a small apartment in Kowloon. It was there that Ani went on her next day off, exiting the Jordan Road subway station clutching the address that Dina had written down on a piece of paper.

Ani found the place on a side street off Austin Road, and took the elevator to the 10th floor. She was greeted at the door by a plain-looking, middle-aged woman, wearing a T-shirt, a plain pair of loose trousers, and rubber flip flops on her feet. She took Ani's jacket and beckoned her to come in.

"Dina told me you could help me," Ani said.

"Yes, I'm sure I can make you feel a lot better. Did Dina, happen to mention . . . ?"

Ani opened her purse, withdrew a single yellow note – one thousand Hong Kong dollars – and handed it to the woman, who crumpled the note in her hand and led Ani inside. They passed a small kitchen, where a young woman was frying something in a wok, and entered one of the bedrooms. It was bare, save for a single bed, a shelf and a plastic closet. The old woman lay down on the bed, propping her shoulders against the wall, while Ani stood by the doorway, uncertain what to do. She instructed Ani to take off her clothes and then motioned Ani to lie down against her body. Ani did as she was directed, lying down nervously on the bed, her weight against the old woman. The woman reached up and took down a bottle of alcohol and some cotton balls. She dabbed the alcohol on a cotton ball and rubbed a spot on Ani's right foot. Then she took down another jar. Inside were thousands of tiny gold needles, no longer than one of Ani's little-finger nails.

The woman started to mumble a prayer, sort of a lullaby. Ani did not understand the dialect, but the words soothed her. She settled back against the woman's warm, ample bosom. "This won't hurt," the woman said. Then she gently but strongly pushed the first needle into the flesh, using a small instrument that looked something like a hammer. Ani felt the prick as the needle broke the flesh, then a burning feeling as the woman pushed the needle deep under the skin.

Ani grimaced and gripped her fists tightly as the woman pushed another needle into the other foot. The torture continued as the woman worked her way up Ani's body, depositing golden needles in her thighs, close to her vagina, in her breasts, and up towards her face. Ani endured all of this stoically, not saying a word. She visibly flinched when the woman started to press needles into her cheekbones. "Nobody will see them, and they won't leave a mark," the woman assured her.

Finally, it was over. Ani lay against the woman's body, staring at the ceiling, not daring to move, until the woman prodded her to get up and put her clothes back on. Stiffly, slowly she rose from the bed, her body tingling from two dozen wounds. She carefully put on her trousers and flannel shirt and walked numbly toward the door.

"I promise you're going to feel much better after this," the woman called from behind, as Ani hurried from the apartment.

But Ani didn't feel any better. She felt terrible. Most of the next day she lay on her cot in agony. It seemed like she suffered a thousand cuts, not just 24. Whatever had persuaded her to let that silly old woman puncture her body in such a painful way? Nothing she promised had transpired. She told her it would not hurt, and it hurt terribly. She told her it would lift her spirits, but she seemed even more depressed than before. The only difference being that instead of thinking constantly about Sumianti, she thought about each one of the 24 golden needles now embedded in her body. She cursed the old woman. She cursed Dina.

Over the next few days the pain continued unabated, and Ani began to grow worried. What if some infection set in? What if she got AIDS! It seemed as if every move she made was painful. It took her three times as long to iron the clothes. Several times her employer looked at her strangely, and once asked if something was wrong. "I'm okay, mam," Ani responded. How could she possibly explain the stupid thing she had done, except possibly to another Indonesian? How could she explain it to anyone?

After suffering for nearly a week, Ani finally decided that she had better seek out real medical treatment. On Sunday, she boarded a bus that took her close to the large public hospital near her home, and joined the crowd of people waiting in the emergency room.

Slowly, Ani emerged from the deep sleep induced by the anesthetic. Groggily she looked around and found herself lying in a bed in the women's ward of the public hospital. She had only a vague memory of being admitted, and the difficulty she had, at first, in trying to explain to the duty doctor what was wrong with her. He seemed to think that she had broken some kind of law against self-mutilation. Then they had sent her for X-rays that clearly showed the tiny metal slivers shining against the blurry black and white background. She slowly lifted her arm and looked at the stitches on the back of her hand. Then she raised her hand to her face. She felt the stitches just above her eyebrows. Her fingers slid down her smooth cheeks. She remembered asking the doctor not to remove the needles there. Vanity prevented her from disfiguring her face. The doctor said she should watch it and come back if she still felt discomfort.

She fell asleep, and a few hours later was awakened by a group of Chinese doctors and interns huddled at the foot of her bed, chattering among themselves. The head doctor pulled out her X-rays and passed them to the others to look at. They studied them with fascination, occasionally lifting their heads to look at Ani. From the snatches of conversation she could make out, it was evident they considered her case very unusual. She drifted off to sleep again. Shortly after dinner, she felt the presence of somebody standing next to her bed. She opened her eyes and looked up at Sumianti.

"How are you feeling Ani?" said Sumianti. Dina heard you had gone to the hospital, but she didn't know which one. It took me a while to find you."

Ani smiled. "I'm okay," she whispered. "It's nice to see you again." Then, hesitatingly, she asked, "where . . . where is your friend?"

"Oh, she was terminated about a week ago."

"Terminated?" Ani whispered. It took her a moment to grasp the implications.

"Yes, she's already gone back to Indonesia."

A few weeks later, Ani and Sumianti were back in Victoria Park, walking together and holding hands. As they walked past the park bench where Dina was sitting, they stopped to chat.

"How are you feeling after your surgery, *mas?*" asked Dina.

"I'm feeling better," Ani replied.

And then, casting a loving glance at Sumianti, she said, "Yes, I'm feeling much better now."

5.

TELEPHONE SEX

Tony closed the door to the love-hotel room and turned the locks. Yuni took off her sweater, and hung it on the brass hook by the door, but she didn't take off any of her other clothes. She looked around the room. She couldn't remember ever being in such a nice place. The woman who had just left, taking Tony's money, was dressed in a pink uniform, like the one worn by the dental assistant, when she took her employer's son to the dentist. A large double bed, neatly made up with a red blanket, dominated the room. It was so big it seemed to Yuni that she could swim in it.

The Chinese family she worked for in Kowloon had only a small apartment, too small even to provide her with a bed of her own, so she shared one with the baby daughter. Still, she was happy enough working in the household, even though the *popo* sometimes nagged and complained that she didn't cook the rice properly. The elderly woman was her almost constant companion – nattering away in Cantonese that Yuni only half understood – since both the husband and his wife spent most of the day working. But her mam had bought her a necklace when she and her husband had returned from a holiday in Thailand.

Tony fussed around the vanity table removing his Rolex watch – stainless steel with a gold band in the middle – his wallet and some loose coins, which made a loud noise as they rattled around on the glass top. He unhooked the mobile phone from his waist and laid it down on the table.

"Do you want the television on?" he asked Yuni. She nodded yes, without moving from where she was standing, close to the door. Tony pushed the button on the set, which was suspended from the ceiling. He spoke in English; it was the language that they used with each other. Yuni's Cantonese was still limited mainly to the phrases she needed to cook the meals and take care of the children – a baby and a ten-year-old boy. Her English was a little better, since she had studied some in high school. A sofa, just large enough for two people, also faced the set, and Yuni walked two steps and settled down on to it. Tony came over and sat down too. The television was tuned to a Chinese soap opera, typical of the televised day fare in Hong Kong. It was the kind of program the *popo* watched all day, while Yuni took care of the baby.

Yuni had met Tony in the park – She went to Victoria Park every Tuesday – It was an odd day of the week for her to have her day off, but her employer needed to take care of the baby on Sundays, when the family went to eat *dim sum*. Yuni usually spent the afternoon sitting on one of the park benches, or wandering among the stores in Causeway Bay, sometimes with her friend Eni, who also had Tuesdays off. In the late afternoon, sometimes she and Eni went to one of the discos in Wanchai that opened early, and spent a couple hours there nursing glasses of orange juice or dancing together on the dance floor.

She was sitting on the park bench one Tuesday, chatting idly with Eni about their employers, when Tony walked by. Something about her look caught his eye, and he stopped and said "hello," and asked if he could sit down beside her for a moment. Eni gave Yuni a nudge, as if to say, "go ahead," and so she gave him an encouraging smile. Tony worked in a nearby high-rise building, so their meetings were in snatches during the day, usually over lunch at a Chinese place, although once, she remembered, he took her, as a special treat, to the Spaghetti House.

Idly watching the TV, Yuni's thoughts drifted back to her home in Indonesia, where she had been a student, until her father's death had forced her to quit her school and come to Hong Kong to work as a domestic helper. There had also been a boy . . .

Her reverie was broken by the insistent beeping of Tony's mobile phone. He heaved himself from the sofa and went over to the vanity table to pick it up. "*Wei*," he whispered quietly into the mouthpiece, in Cantonese. Yuni, making out snatches of the conversation, could tell he was talking to his wife. It was something he did frequently when they were together, much to

Yuni's annoyance. Tony finished the conversation, closed the phone, placed it back on the counter and came back to the sofa.

"I wish you would turn your phone off when we're together," she said. "I can't do that. My wife might wonder what I was doing and get suspicious." Yuni said nothing more, and they both stared silently for several minutes at the soap opera, as if they were absorbed in its absurd situations. Then Tony got up and pushed the channel buttons, tuning it to a taped blue movie. Tony came back to the sofa, removed his coat and lay it out on the bed. He draped his arm around Yuni's shoulder, one finger playing tentatively with her breast.

Yuni watched the television screen in the same mute silence, and did nothing to encourage any further exploration. She had seen blue movies before, but not until she had moved to Hong Kong. Her friend Eni had a television and VCR in her small bedroom and the two of them sometimes spent part of their day off watching them. Eni even had a video store membership card.

Tony's phone rang again. He removed his hand from her breast, moved over to the vanity table, and turned the volume on the television down. He whispered urgently into the mouthpiece. Yuni could understand very little of what they said. It almost seemed as if Tony's wife knew about their meetings, by some kind of mental telepathy. Irritably, he snapped the phone shut and turned the volume on the television back up again. Instead of returning to the sofa, he lay down on the bed, putting his arms around his head and staring at the video. He didn't say anything or invite her to join him, and Yuni didn't move from the sofa. The two sat in silence, the only sounds, the steady hum of the air conditioner and the naked rhythms emanating from the screen.

Yuni was startled to hear a phone go off again, although this time it had a different tone. Tony reached over to the side table and picked up the receiver, not bothering to give a greeting, and then dropped it back on the cradle. "They said the time is up," he said.

She got up from the sofa and walked into the bathroom. She looked at her unmussed face in the mirror above the wash basin, took out a lipstick from her purse and dabbed some on her mouth, an unnecessary gesture, really. On the shelf, wrapped in cellophane was a brown plastic comb. Yuni took it out of the wrapping and held the heavy object in her hand, admiring its color and feel. She casually ran the teeth through her hair. It was, in fact, a very nice comb. She turned to Tony, who was framed in the doorway, putting on his jacket. "Do you think they would let me take this with me?"

"Why didn't you take the phone out of his hands and tell his wife not to bother you?" said Dina an hour later. They were sitting on a bench in the park. Tony had gone back to his office.

"Oh, I could never do that. What would I have said to her?"

"Maybe it would have got Tony to turn off his mobile phone when he is in bed with you."

"But it might have got him in a lot of trouble."

At that moment, Dina's own phone started ringing. She fished in her handbag, brought it out and spoke into the mouthpiece. With the phone in her ear, she fished around again in the bag, pulling out a bunch of phonecards. She detached one from the pile, scratched it with her fingernail, and read out the numbers over the phone, then snapped it shut and resumed talking to Yuni.

They fell into silence. Dina's mobile rang again, and again she spoke with another woman, this time about sending some money back to Indonesia. That reminded Yuni that she needed to give Dina some money to send back to her mother. She had placed two bank notes in her wallet for this purpose. Nestled next to it in her bag was her own mobile phone, inert, silent during the afternoon. She reached in, pulled it out, and fingered it quietly in the palm of her hand. She turned her head to Dina. "Do you think he will call?"

6.

DINA

Sometimes, out of sheer restlessness, Dina left her small apartment after midnight and roamed the streets of Causeway Bay. Even at that hour there was still a lot of life in this part of Hong Kong. As she walked down Paterson Street, she ran into a group of Chinese people leaving the last show at the cinema. She turned past the Sogo department store. Its steel door shutters were drawn down, but people were still coming and going into the nearby subway exit, a slight hurry in their steps, to catch the last train before the service shut down for the night.

Dina crossed Hennessy Road and walked behind the Mitsukoshi department store. She turned down an alley, which housed a night market. The string of overhead light bulbs was still lit, but most of the stalls were closing, the owners packing the T-shirts and jeans away for another night. At the far end of the alley, she saw the light glowing over a fruit stand. She walked down to it and picked over the offerings. She thought about buying a plump mango for breakfast, but decided it was too heavy to carry around. Instead, she pointed to some lychee nuts. The owner placed them in a plastic sack, accepted the ten dollars and handed the sack to Dina.

She crossed Hennessy Road again and entered Victoria Park. The old men playing checkers under the floodlights had gone home. But the night was warm, and people were still in the park. Dina walked past couples necking on the park benches in the shadows. She continued past the model-boat pool and the Thai restaurant, now closed, and climbed a little knoll. She sat down on a bench, placing the sack of lychee nuts down beside her. She took one of the nuts out, split the skin using both of her thumbs and plumped the pulp into her mouth. Across the yacht basin flickered the lights of distant Kowloon.

When Dina first came to Hong Kong, nearly ten years ago, to work as a domestic helper, she had lived in Kowloon. In those earlier days she saw very little of Hong Kong. It was six months before she even took the Star Ferry across the harbor to Hong Kong side. A year later she had earned Sundays off, and she spent them cutting hair – a skill she learned in Indonesia – among the thousands of Filipina maids gathered in Statue Square on their day off. As the number of Indonesian women working in Hong Kong began to grow, she shifted to Victoria Park and added other businesses: changing money; selling magazines and phonecards.

She discarded the last lychee shell in her plastic bag, got up from the park bench, walked over to the trash receptacle and tossed the bag in. She leaned up against the railing for a few moments, then walked down the steps and out of the park, past the Park Lane Hotel. Even at this hour – now well past midnight – people were still coming and going through the big front entrance. She found her own street and walked back to the entrance of Garden Mansions, where she maintained a one-room apartment.

The next morning – she did every morning after awakening – she took a lengthy shower in the tiny cubicle that doubled as a toilet. She dressed and applied her makeup. Then she grabbed her handbag and a large plastic bag filled with magazines and walked the few blocks to the park. She spent the day there, her hand bag stuffed with rupiah and phonecards, her plastic bag full of magazines. On Sundays, she still cut hair all day, from a spot in front of the yacht basin. These small businesses brought in enough money to allow her to buy a home and several hectares of farmland back in Indonesia. Lately, however, she had started a new business, and it was this business that was keeping her up at night.

Dina exited the subway entrance and turned down Lockhart Road to the Makati Disco. She climbed the stairs, pushed through the rope curtain and entered the room, pausing near the entrance to survey the scene. Ignoring the Western men sitting around the bar, nursing drinks and staring at the women, she looked closely at the women on the dance floor or leaning against the walls, or in the dark recesses of the disco, searching for one woman in particular. In one corner of the bar, sitting under a pool of light and nursing a glass of orange juice, she spotted Wiji and walked over to her. Wiji greeted her a big smile.

"I don't usually see you here. Are you meeting somebody?"

"I'm looking for Ivy. Have you seen her?"

"Ivy?" Wiji turned the name over in her mind. At first she couldn't place it. Then she remembered.

"Oh, I know. She's the one that works in a coffee shop and was married to that English guy. I think they separated, but she still has a dependent's visa. Sometimes I see her here, but not tonight. But then it's a little early." She paused for a while. "Why do you want to see her?"

"She owes me money," said Dina, looking around the disco again.

"Look, why not stay here for a while and have a drink?"

Dina hesitated. She was working. Then she thought, why not? And settled on to the bar stool. Wiji signaled the waitress, who was a friend of hers, and the waitress placed a complimentary glass of orange juice in front of Dina. She picked it up and took a sip.

Wiji looked at Dina appraisingly. She was attractive in a quiet way. She dressed conservatively compared with the other maids out on the town that night, with their tank tops, bare shoulders, and tight jeans. Her hair was cut short, but tastefully, befitting a woman who earned part of her living cutting other women's hair. She could easily have been taken for an office worker, perhaps a receptionist, Wiji wondered if she had a boyfriend.

Before she could say anything, however, Sussy joined them, flinging her handbag expertly on the counter and hiking her body onto the bar stool. She was dressed for work, with a halter top and tight jeans. Her dyed blond hair gleamed under the bar lights. She glanced over at Dina. "What brings you here? You're not out cruising are you?" she said archly.

"I'm looking for Ivy. Have you seen her?"

"Ivy? I think I saw her at the Big Apple, a little while ago. Why? Are you looking for her?"

"She owes me money,"

"I hear everybody owes you money." Sussy said, looking in the direction of a Western man sitting further down the bar. He stared back at her and lifted his glass in greeting. "Maybe I should get in that business."

"Stick with your own hustle," Dina advised. Really, it's a struggle. I've called Ivy over and over, and she won't even answer her mobile phone. I went to her place but she wouldn't answer the door. I'm not sure what to do."

"You know, Ivy has a son back in Indonesia, from her ex-husband . . ."

"I know," Dina cut in. "That's why she borrowed fifteen thousand dollars from me. She had to pay the fees at his convent school. She still owes me three thousand."

"What I meant to say is . . . her son is technically an overstay. They never registered him with Immigration. You could threaten to have your sister call Immigration in Indonesia and report her. I bet she would pay pretty quickly if you did that."

Dina turned the idea over in her mind. She was tempted. She was tired of trying to cajole or bully Ivy into paying. It would be nice to have something over her. But Immigration was a double-edged sword. Dina was vulnerable herself, since she paid a Chinese man to pose as her employer so she could stay in Hong Kong. Ivy could easily turn her into the authorities.

The Western man had by now sidled closer to the cluster of three women. Dina ignored him, but Sussy gave him a warm smile and started a conversation. Dina decided that it was time to leave. She swallowed the last of her orange juice, heaved herself off the bar stool and waved goodbye.

Outside the disco she turned west and walked to the intersection. Sussy said she had seen Ivy at the Big Apple, so she crossed Lockhart Road, walking by the cluster of hookers sitting by the noodle stand. A boisterous group of American sailors exited the bar next to it, one of them slightly brushing Dina as she strode along. "Excuse me lady, say . . ." said one of the sailors, but Dina ignored him, walking straight ahead until she came to an entrance with a big neon sign above it. She descended the stairs into the darkness.

The Big Apple was not crowded, and it didn't take Dina long to determine that Ivy was not there either. She was about to leave when she felt an arm grab her. She turned around and looked at Retno.

"Where are you going? I don't usually see you here," Retno said.

Dina did not particularly like Retno. She spent most of her days hanging around Victoria Park, usually with Wati and her group. But Retno knew a lot of people, so Dina decided to linger a while.

"I'm looking for Ivy. Sussy said she saw her in the Big Apple. You haven't seen her have you?"

"I think I saw her here a little while ago, but she left with some other women. Why are you looking for her?"

"She owes me money, and I can't find her to get her to pay up," Dina replied.

Retno thought this over. "Come on, sit down for a while. Buy me a drink. Maybe I can help you." Dina set her handbag on the floor and eased onto the barstool. She motioned the bartender for two orange juices. Retno sidled up next to her. She seemed in a mood to talk.

"What you need is a way to frighten her into paying," Retno said. "You know. Like some of the Chinese guys who get money from you in the park."

Dina knew what she was talking about. Sometimes the triads demanded money to allow her to sell things. She usually paid them since they only demanded small sums, a hundred here, two hundred there.

"Ahmed has some friends. Maybe I could try to call him. I'll bet they could persuade Ivy to pay up pretty quick . . ." Ahmed was Retno's ex-boyfriend, a burly Pakistani who worked as a doorman at a luxury hotel in Kowloon.

"I thought you two broke up a long time ago. How can Ahmed help, if you don't even know how to contact him. Anyway, it might get him in trouble."

Dina downed her orange juice and climbed the stairs out of the disco, into the warm night. She walked down Lockhart Road, stopping one by one at the rest of the discos, but she couldn't find Ivy. Finally, she gave up and took the subway back to Causeway Bay.

It was past midnight, and Dina couldn't sleep. She thought about going out for a walk, but her legs still ached slightly from her exertions in Wanchai. She turned her television on, thinking it might lull her to sleep. The Hong Kong station was playing an American gangster program, and Dina gradually became absorbed in the action. On the screen two burly men were hovering over another man. One man gripped his arm firmly behind his back. "You don't pay up, we're gonna break your arm," he said. Dina repeated the phrase out loud in English, "You don't pay and I'm going to break your arm." She smiled at the sound of it. She imagined Ahmed's friends standing over Ivy, twisting her arm behind her back. "If you don't pay up, we're going to break your arm." And Ivy's trembling hands, reaching into her bag and pulling out the bank notes.

Dina watched until the program ended. The gangsters had been captured and were in police custody. The camera lingered on a wanted poster pinned on the police wall that showed an unsmiling mug. A uniformed arm reached up and ripped the poster off the wall. "The End" appeared on the screen, along with the credits. Soon after, Dina fell asleep.

As soon as she awoke the next morning, she began to rummage through her cabinet for an old shoe box where she hid the passports that she kept as a form of collateral. She pulled out Ivy's passport and opened it, looking at the unsmiling photograph. She put it in her handbag and got dressed.

She took the passport to a shop that had a photocopier machine. She opened the document to the photo, closed the top of the machine and pushed the button, watching the copy with Ivy's photo fall into the tray. Then she took out a black felt tip pen, sat down at one of the desks and carefully lettered the page.

WARNING
Sukemi Rohani
"Ivy"
Won't Pay Her Debts

Then she put the document back in the copier.

That afternoon she went to the coffee shop where Ivy worked. She saw her standing behind the counter, but she did not go inside. Dina began passing her flyers out to people as they entered the coffee shop. They gave it a puzzled look as they entered. Ivy eyed Dina nervously from behind the counter. Then she slipped away, as if waiting on a customer, and picked up one of the flyers that had been left on the table. She went outside to Dina.

"What do you think you're doing? Do you want to get me fired?"

Dina ignored her and handed another flyer to somebody entering the coffee shop. Ivy snatched it out of his hand.

"I'll get the manager," Ivy said.

"Go ahead. I'll give him one too," Dina replied.

Ivy stormed back into the coffee shop and soon after that Dina left.

The next Saturday Dina was sitting on the curb under the big tree. She was busy, and didn't notice Ivy until she was standing directly in front of her. Wordlessly, Ivy opened her handbag and pulled out three yellow thousand-dollar notes and handed them to Dina. She took the money, pushed it deep into her purse, pulled out the passport and handed it over. Ivy turned and walked away. Dina watched as she disappeared out of the park. Then she stood up and turned around with a satisfied smile on her face. Behind her she had pinned one of the "Wanted"

posters on the trunk of the tree. She reached up and ripped the
poster off of the tree.

7.

SUSSY'S WORLD

Sussy danced alone, slowly undulating in front of the full-length mirror mounted on a post at the edge of the dance floor. A middle-aged Western man turned his body half away from the bar so that he could watch her. Sussy looked over in his direction, and he smiled at her. But Sussy turned her attention back to the mirror, admiring herself in the reflection. She was dressed in her best white jeans, with a red halter top, which nicely accentuated her figure. She was a pretty woman, about 28. She had dyed her hair blond, with some brown streaks in it. It gave her a kind of ghost-like appearance, set against the darkness of her complexion. But she believed that customers found it titillating, especially the Western men who frequented the Makati disco. She continued dancing in front of the mirror, lost in her own private narcissism.

The Western man was already gone when Sussy, finally tired of dancing by herself, went to the far corner of the bar and hiked her hips onto the bar stool. Imelda, the Filipina bartender, placed a glass of orange juice in front of her without waiting to be asked. When drinking by herself, Sussy confined herself to orange juice or soft drinks. She allowed men to buy her margaritas or tequilas – for which the disco charged an outrageous price – half of which went to Sussy.

She always sat at the corner of the bar, where she could see everything that was going on in the disco. It was late, and only a handful of Filipina women were dancing by themselves on the small dance floor. A few Western men sat around the bar. Two of them, both wearing business suits, were sitting on the opposite side from her. Sussy stared directly at them, but they ignored her and continued talking among themselves. Sussy looked back down at her orange juice and took another a long pull, since she was thirsty from her exertions.

Imelda came over to Sussy's corner, and said, "kind of quiet tonight."

"Well, the US Navy is coming into town soon," said Sussy. "I heard they are due here next week. A big ship, an aircraft carrier. Lots of sailors. We could use the business." Somehow, the Wanchai intelligence service always knew when the American ships were arriving.

"We had a raid last night, just after you left," Imelda said, changing the subject.

Sussy turned her head away from a Western guy who had just entered the disco. "What kind of raid, Immigration?"

"Yes, three officers and a woman came in. They stopped the music and examined everyone's ID, even me. I think they took three women away with them."

"You say after I left. What time?"

"I think it was around eleven-thirty."

Sussy remembered that she had left with a young man from Taiwan around 11 p.m. If not for him she might have been taken in herself. She shuddered at the thought. Like most of the Indonesian women who stalked Wanchai, Sussy was an overstay. Her domestic-helper visa had expired more than a year before, after she had been terminated, and had not been able to find another employer. She lived in a small boarding house in Wanchai, which she shared with three other women, two of whom were overstays like herself.

"Didn't you get any warning?" Sussy asked.

"No. The band had taken a break." Sometimes the management passed word of an impending raid to the Filipino band, and they sing-songed a warning in Tagalog, after which a good part of the customers clambered down the stairs and disappeared.

A lone German man, sitting at the bar, looked over at Sussy and smiled. Sussy smiled back at him. "Buy a drink for the lady?" Imelda prompted from behind the bar. "Okay," he said. Imelda retreated back into the bar to pour a margarita, perfect teamwork.

"Shouldn't we move over to the table?" said Sussy, as Imelda placed the drink in front of her and whispered "one hundred and sixty" to the German man. He pulled a couple red notes out of his wallet and handed them over. Sussy had already moved in the direction of the sofa at the far side of the dance floor while he got his change.

The man placed his beer on the table and sat down. Sussy sat beside him and snuggled close to his side. He put a large hand on her thigh. Sussy took a sip from her margarita. It tasted bitter – Sussy didn't like the taste of alcohol. The man sat silently, staring at the women who were on the dance floor. Sussy searched her mind for a subject to open a conversation, but before she could open her mouth, the man asked, "you are a Filipina?"

"No, I'm from Indonesia," Sussy replied. That seemed to exhaust the conversation. The band finished its set and moved off the stage to take a break. The man said nothing more, but kept his hand resting on Sussy's thigh. At that moment Lula walked into the disco and moved toward the bar. Sussy followed her with her eyes. A few moments later, the German heaved himself from the sofa. "I must go," he said and walked out of the disco, with only a nod in Sussy's direction. Sussy immediately got up and walked over to Lula, leaving her drink behind her on the table.

"Hi," she said to her friend, while accepting a drink chit from Imelda and putting it in her purse. Lula, a Filipina, was a plump, partridge of a woman, loaded with bangles and dangling earrings. She wore red shorts, and the edges cut into her plump thighs. She was already involved in a complicated story with Imelda, . . . "and so I told him to get lost."

"Told who to get lost?" asked Sussy, as she sat down on the bar stool.

"This police superintendent I've been seeing."

Lulu then launched into the story again. She had met this British police officer at the disco about one week previously, and they had gone out together for three nights. Lula began to think of him as her boyfriend.

"He has his own car, and he drove me back to his place."

"Where was that?" Sussy interjected.

"I'm not sure. Somewhere in the New Territories, I think. It was dark, and we had to drive a long time. And anyway I was a little drunk," she continued. "When we got to his house I was surprised. He had all of these weird devices, like chains and ropes and things, in his bedroom. He told me he wanted to have me chain him to the bedpost with his handcuffs. I didn't know what to do. Nobody ever asked me to do that. And I was way out in the country."

"Maybe you should have called the police," said Sussy.

The two women giggled. Imelda had moved away to serve a customer.

"I told him I didn't want to do that, and he said, okay, and so we just had some more drinks, and got into bed."

"The next night I came into the disco at the right time, and I saw him sitting and drinking with another girl. I thought maybe he was just waiting for me, but he didn't move away from her, even though I knew he could see me. Then he called me over and asked me to sit down beside him. He bought me a drink. I thought he would send the other woman away, but he didn't."

"Then do you know what?"

Sussy just looked back at her.

"He asked me to go home with him and the other woman," she said indignantly.

Sussy smiled and said, "why didn't you ask me. I would have gone with the two of you?"

"Why? Do you want to be on the top or the bottom," Lula replied. They both laughed.

"Well, anyway, he left with that woman, and I haven't seen him since."

They fell silent for a few moments, and surveyed the disco scene. A few more middle-aged Western men had settled around the bar, and Lula turned her attention to them. They were talking to younger women. Sussy didn't recognize them, and assumed they were domestic helpers with a free night.

Lula's story had got Sussy thinking about her own "boyfriend." His name was John and he was an American sailor in his early twenties. When his ship had paid a port call in Hong Kong three months previously, Sussy had spent nearly a week with him, living at the hotel where he stayed before his ship returned to Japan.

Sussy kept in touch with him through e-mail. Once or twice a week she went to Nurma's Place and rented one of the computers, so that she and John could chat with each other online. He sent her brief messages about his life aboard his ship, while Sussy twitted him good-naturedly about his Japanese girlfriends – which he strenuously denied having. Sussy did not believe this, but she was surprised at how excited she felt when he told her that his ship was returning to Hong Kong.

Lula had moved away from Sussy and was chatting with one of the men sitting at the bar. A few moments later the two of them got up and moved toward one of the sofas. Lula gave Sussy a small wave. Sussy sat drinking alone. Several of the men sitting along the bar got up and walked out of the disco. The Filipina band swung into a spirited rendition of "Angelina." Sussy looked to see if Lula and her new partner were on the dance floor, but she couldn't find her.

Fifteen minutes later Lula came back to the bar, and, snatching the drinks chit offered by Imelda, said to Sussy, "Let's go someplace else. This place is dead." Sussy nodded and retrieved her handbag from behind the bar. Lula was already stalking out of the disco, and she had to hurry to catch up with her. They emerged on Lockhart Road, hit by the heat from the summer's evening. They walked down the street, past the topless bars with their tired Chinese touts sitting on the stoop trying to entice in any of the Western men passing along. In front of the doors, fires flickered in tin trays, an offering to a Chinese deity. "Where do you want to go next?" Sussy asked, as they came to the intersection. "Maybe we should try the Neptune."

"I don't like that place. It's filled with hookers from Thailand and China. You can hardly find a place to sit around the bar."

"Okay, let's go to the Big Apple," Sussy responded. The two crossed Lockhart Road and walked a couple of blocks to the entrance. The Chinese man manning the podium at the entrance recognized them and waved them into the disco's glowing darkness. Sussy looked around, her eyes adjusting to the darkness, listening to the beat of another Filipino band. They walked over to the bar and sat down on the stools. Sussy passed her handbag over to the bartender and ordered an orange juice. "Why did you leave that guy so soon?" she inquired.

"He was an asshole." Lula replied, but said no more. She dug into her handbag and pulled out a packet of cigarettes, extracted one and lit it. Sussy grimaced. She hated the smell of cigarette smoke, and Lula usually didn't smoke when they were together. They both looked over the disco scene. The dance floor was thinning out. Only about a half a dozen women danced together. There were only a handful of men. "We should have stayed at the other place," Sussy ventured, but Lula didn't respond. She just took another drag on her cigarette and stared at the dance floor.

"You know, I don't have enough to pay my rent. I'm still a couple hundred short. I was about to order another drink with that guy at the other place, when that Francisca woman came over and sat down beside him. Now all I have is this," she pulled one crumpled drinks chit out of her purse. Francisca was another Filipina PR girl, younger and prettier than Lula. She was well known in the discos for stealing customers from the other girls in the bar. She had done it to Sussy too.

A few minutes later, two Chinese women, both tall and svelte, entered the disco and walked over to the bar. One of them sat down on the bar stool while the other stood beside her and fixed the two men sitting nearby with a stare.

"Northern mushrooms," Lula said, using a common term for Chinese prostitutes who came into Hong Kong on tourist visas and stayed for two weeks, making more money than they would in a year working in a textile factory.

"Why don't they stay at the Neptune where they belong?" Lula said crossly.

"Maybe things were dead there, just like here," Sussy replied. After a few minutes, the two men sitting at the bar got up and moved over to where the Chinese women were, and started to talk in a low murmur. Then they all left the disco together. Lula followed them with her eyes.

Lula turned her attention back to Sussy. She noticed that Sussy had taken three drinks chits out of her purse and placed them on the counter, next to Lula's drink.

"What's this?"

"Here, you take them. I don't need them. John is coming to Hong Kong in a couple days. He'll take care of me. He's very generous."

Lula looked at the drinks chits for a few moments. Then she slowly picked them up and put them in her purse.

"Come on, she said. Let's go someplace else. I don't like it here."

Sussy nodded in agreement. The disco was getting emptier. She looked at her watch. It was nearly 4 a.m. The two climbed the stairs and emerged on Luard Road.

"Where do you want to go now?" Sussy asked. "The Strawberry?"

"I don't know. It gets pretty crowded at this hour. All of the girls from the topless bars, who haven't been bought out, go there looking for a late date." Sussy knew that. She often ended the night there too.

They passed by a barbecue stall, and suddenly Sussy felt very hungry. "Let's get something," she said. Lula gave her a look. "I'll pay." She pointed to the beef sizzling on a stick, raised two fingers and handed the vendor twenty dollars. She handed one of the skewers to Lula and kept one for herself. Then they continued walking down the street.

They spotted Dina, sitting on the stoop in front of the 7-Eleven Store. Dina often came to Wanchai in the early-morning hours, changing money for the Indonesian women who had had a successful night, loaning money to those who had come up dry.

"How are things going tonight, *mbak?*" she greeted Sussy cheerfully. Sussy decided to linger a while and talk. Lula hesitated then said, "I think I'll go to the Strawberry. You can stay here." Then she gave a short wave and walked down the street.

"You aren't going to the Strawberry?" Dina inquired, as Sussy sat down on the stoop next to her. She offered Dina a taste from her skewer, but Dina shook her head, no.

"Slow night in Wanchai," Dina said.

"Yes, I only had three drinks this evening. I think Lula had only one. I gave her my chits. She's getting behind on the rent."

"You don't need them?"

"I'm okay for now. What about you?"

"One woman came by to change a thousand-dollar note. She must have had a pretty good night."

Sussy was impressed, "I wonder which disco she was working in. Everywhere I went tonight, it seemed pretty dead."

A few moments later Retno walked by. She was wearing her usual grubby man's shirt, rolled up at the sleeves. Her unhealthy, pasty face was devoid of makeup. Dina suspected that she took drugs, but wondered where she got the money for them, since she didn't have many customers. Having no permanent place to live, Retno hung around Wanchai at night, sleeping in the booths of all-night discos. Since Retno did not owe Dina any money for the moment, Dina was inclined to be friendly.

"Sit down, *mbak*," she said. Sussy silently offered her the last piece of beef on the stick. Retno squatted down and accepted the skewer, eating greedily.

"Any luck tonight?" Sussy asked. She shook her head and discarded the stick among the burnt-out ashes of the tin tray on the stoop, wiping her mouth on her sleeve.

"The US Navy is coming to Hong Kong in a few days," Sussy said.

"Oh?" Retno perked up. Almost the only time she picked up a customer was when the discos were full of sailors. She appealed to some of the shyer ones, who felt a little intimidated by the flashier Filipinas or the haughty Chinese. For a while she had a regular boyfriend, but he had been transferred, and no longer came to Hong Kong.

Sussy stood and picked up her handbag. "Are you going over to Strawberry?" Dina asked.

"No, I think I'll call it a night. Bye." She gave the two women a small wave and started walking down the street. In a few more days the navy would be in town, John with them. They would have nearly a whole week together. It was something to look forward to.

8.

SITI'S ESCAPE

Siti plotted her escape as she lay on her cot in the dank basement storeroom that doubled as her bedroom. It was late and she was exhausted after having finished her last household chore. She could hear water steadily dripping against the bare concrete wall as she lay waiting for the last member of the family to take a shower before taking hers. The coursing warm water would ease somewhat the ache in her small bones that came from washing clothes, fixing meals and cleaning toilets for 18 hours each day.

She was a woman of 24, and was not totally inexperienced in the difficulties and humiliations of being a maid in a large Chinese household. She had come to Hong Kong six months previously after having worked for two years in Singapore. But that experience had not prepared her for the difficulties that she had encountered after coming to Hong Kong. It wasn't just the constant verbal abuse that the old *popo* heaped on her when she spoiled the rice. Nor was it her mam's constant criticism over the way she ironed her husband's shirts. That was pretty standard.

What really grated on her was the fact that after working 18 hours a day, with only one day off a month, she was not making any money. Of course, she was still in debt to the agency that had found her the job. Worse, her employer paid her only half the minimum wage, even though the mam required her every month to sign a receipt that stated that she had received the full wages owed her by contract and stipulated by law. She suspected that her agency pocketed the difference.

Sometimes she fished her bank book out of the bottom of the small suitcase where she kept most of her clothes and what other small possessions she had brought with her. She looked at the numbers that never seemed to grow – precisely HK$1,342.25. There were three entries, each for 200 dollars, since she had come to Hong Kong. The rest was what was left of the little she had accumulated in Singapore. She did not have to send money back to her family, as so many others did, so there was no reason why she couldn't begin to save more. Maybe even accumulate enough to buy a home back in Indonesia. But only if she was paid a fair wage.

She knew that it was possible. On her rare holidays, she had met some other Indonesian women in Victoria Park who had managed to accumulate a tidy sum while working in Hong Kong. Of course, they all worked for employers who paid them full, fair wages, gave them weekly holidays and otherwise lived up to their contracts. How, she wondered, could she find an employer like that. To ask her agency for help was useless.

"You're lucky to have any job. There are thousands of girls just like you who want to take your place. Stop complaining, or they might terminate you," Mr. Chan had said, the last time she had visited her agency. Anyway, she strongly suspected that they were in league with the employers.

Siti wrestled with her problem as she lay on her cot. She could quit her job, but that would mean having to go back to Indonesia. If she ever wanted to get another job in Hong Kong, she would have to enslave herself to another agency.

"It's so unfair," Siti said, explaining the situation to Dina. They were sitting together in Victoria Park on one of Siti's rare days off.

"I heard about a family in Kowloon that wants an experienced helper. Their maid is going back home soon to get married," Dina said. "Maybe you could apply. I know they pay a full wage."

"How can I sign a new contract when the agency still has my passport?" Siti replied.

Before Dina could respond, a woman came up to Dina – who often doubled as a travel agent. She dug into her purse, pulled out an airline ticket, and began going over the itinerary of the woman's flight to Jakarta the next day.

"Her mother's sick, and she is going home to be with her," Dina explained after the woman had taken the ticket and walked back toward Causeway Bay.

"I'm surprised her employer let her go," said Siti, but already a plan was beginning to form in her mind. Maybe she could take the job that Dina had told her about. But only if she could get her hands on the passport. Before returning to her home she bought a phonecard from Dina, and that evening she snuck out of the house and called her sister in Indonesia from a local 7-11 store.

About one week later a letter arrived. The mam rather brusquely handed the envelope to Siti, as if the foreign mail was some kind of invasion of her home. Siti took it to her sleeping area, casually opened the envelope, and read the contents. They described the most routine family matters: her brother had bought a used motorcycle; Her father's arthritis was hurting him again. When the mam returned from work, Siti took the letter to her, putting on a mournful face. She even tried to generate a few tears.

"Mam, I have this letter from home," she began haltingly. "It's some bad news from my home. My mother is very sick. My sister says she might die. They want me to come home to see her right away."

She flourished the letter in front of her employer for a moment without speaking further, and then her mam grabbed it out of her hands, staring at the Indonesian words without comprehension. Siti waited a few moments, expectantly.

"Why you need to go home?"

"Well, you see . . . my mother . . . I'll only be away for a little while, maybe one week."

"I don't know. Who will take care of the baby while you are gone?"

"I think maybe I can get my cousin to come over once or twice while I'm gone."

"I better ask my husband."

It went on like this for several minutes before the woman finally and grudgingly agreed that she could go home, but not for more than one week. She never once asked for any details about the condition of her mother.

Next Siti borrowed a couple thousand dollars from her cousin and bought a round-trip airline ticket from Dina. She also bought a large plastic bag with blue and white stripes on it and stuffed it with rags and old newspapers. No one ever went back to Indonesia without taking clothes and other presents for the family. It would have looked strange to the agency if she had carried only the small suitcase that held virtually all of her belongings. She hoped after she had packed it that her mam would not notice that she had taken everything she owned. But then she never looked into her shabby sleeping area. The ticket lay triumphantly on top of the cot. She had everything she needed – except her passport.

On the day she was to leave, Siti wrestled the plastic bag and suitcase onto the bus, taking two seats for herself. It required two bus changes before she arrived at the airport. She found a trolley, placed her bags on it and pushed it in the direction of the Garuda Airlines counter, scanning the hall for the woman from the agency. "She'll meet you at the check-in counter," she was told. The woman had her passport and a letter for Immigration, explaining why she had to return home so suddenly.

After a few moments, Siti spotted the woman. She had seen her before at the agency, when she first arrived in Hong Kong. The woman gave her a curt greeting, and said, "let's get checked in. You don't have that much time." It didn't look like she wanted to waste time hanging around the airport.

The two women did not speak again, as the line moved slowly towards the check-in counter. Nor did she hand over the passport, which must have been sitting in her handbag. At the counter the ticketing agent asked Siti if she wanted to check in any luggage, and she wrestled the big plastic bag onto the scale, leaving her smaller suitcase by the counter.

"Just the one?" asked the ticketing agent.

"Yes, I want to carry this one with me. It has some clothes I want to change into on the airplane," she said hastily." The woman from the agency said nothing.

"May I see your passport, please," said the ticketing agent.

Only at that moment did the woman from the agency reach into her bag and hand the precious green document to the ticketing agent. She also pulled out the letter and gave it to Siti. She still said nothing more.

The ticket agent flipped through the pages, glanced at Siti and then handed the passport to her. She grasped it firmly in her hand.

"Your gate number is 24. They're boarding now, so you better go straight to the immigration counter and check in."

Siti showed her boarding pass to the gate guard and entered the immigration hall. The woman from the agency stood by the gate. You could tell that she would have liked to follow Siti to the immigration counter, but she had no boarding pass.

Once inside, Siti looked for the longest line she could find – happily at the far end of the hall – and got in the back, fingering her passport in one hand. She glanced back at the gate but could not tell if the woman from the agency was still waiting outside. She still had about 40 minutes until the flight to Jakarta was scheduled to depart. She was only two passengers away from the immigration counter, when she abruptly left the line and went back to the far end. A couple of other passengers waiting in the line, looked at her with some curiosity.

She nervously inched her suitcase forward as the line slowly moved toward the immigration counter, occasionally glancing at her watch and casting another look toward the gate where she had entered. As she approached the end of the counter, she took another look at her watch and at the gate. Deciding one more time, for safety's sake, she again pulled out of the line and moved into another one that was a little bit longer.

Finally, Siti abruptly exited the line and headed for the gate. The woman from the agency was gone. As she walked back into the departure hall, the security guard put out a restraining arm. "Where are you going?" he asked. "Let me see your boarding pass." She flashed it in front of him, and mumbled something about having to get some documents from the woman that was here a minute ago.

"Your flight leaves in only twenty minutes," he said.

"I'll only be five minutes," she said breaking free of his arm and rushing into the departure hall. She looked around again, nervously, but the woman from the agency was nowhere to be seen. Clutching her suitcase, she headed to the front of the hall and down the stairs to the arrival hall, where the taxis were located. She got into the long line, fingering her passport in one hand as she slowly moved toward the line of waiting taxis. When she finally got to the front, she heaved her small suitcase onto the back seat and climbed in, giving the driver the address in Causeway Bay of her new employer. As the cab slowly pulled away from the airport, she sank back into the seat, clutching her passport to her breast, her heart pounding, sweating from fear and relief. "Free at last," she said. "I'm free at last."

9.

THE BALINESE DANCE SOCIETY

They had their own amateur drama society. It was called the Balinese Dance Society, although nobody in it was Balinese; all of the women came from Java. Miriam was the only member of the group who had actually been to Bali, where she worked as a waitress at a tourist hotel in Denpasar before moving to Hong Kong to work on a cruise liner. They met on Sundays in Victoria Park, where they planted a tape recorder on the concrete football pitch. The Gamelan music blared out of the box. The women – the group varied from six to eight, usually – went through the motions of the dance, with perhaps more enthusiasm than grace. Then they broke out plastic sheets and lunch boxes and spent much of the rest of the afternoon eating, gossiping and laughing, like thousands of other women on their day off.

The Balinese dances she saw at the tourist hotel had fascinated Miriam. She had a large collection of music tapes, which she kept in the cabin that she shared with another Indonesian woman on the ship, and she often played them while her cabin mate was on duty. Sometimes, while lying in her bunk, Miriam dreamed about putting on a real dance performance before a real audience. She imagined her friends in shimmering silk sarongs, their faces made up beautifully, the golden headdresses on their heads, the clanging of the cymbals and the banging of the drums. For a moment she thought about asking the cruise line to let her put on a performance for the passengers, but that would have been difficult since most of the members of the Balinese Dance Society could not get away for the two or three days that the ship was at sea during the week.

One day Miriam was sitting in the park next to Dina. It was a mid-week day, and her cruise ship was in port. The other members of the Balinese Dance Society were working.

"I hear there is going to be an Asian Arts Festival next month at Queen Elizabeth Stadium," said Dina

"Oh?" Miriam's attention perked up. "Where did you hear that?"

"At the Consulate. I think they are looking for groups to take part in the festival. Otherwise, it will be dominated by the Filipinas. Why don't you put your dance group on the program? I think they would be happy to have you participate."

"I don't know. The girls have never performed before." Then she brightened, "could you help us?"

"I'll talk to them. Give me your phone number."

Siti and Zuhriah were enthusiastic when Miriam told the Balinese Dance Society, the following Sunday, what she had heard from Dina.

"I'd love to wear one of those gorgeous costumes," said Siti.

"But where are we going to find the materials, and who is going to make them for us?" said Dwi.

"Maybe we could make them ourselves," said Emi.

"I'd like to do it, but what time would we put on the performance. You know I have a curfew," said Leila.

"Why don't we just do a *dangdug* dance?" suggested Zuhriah, who started twirling and shimmering by herself. The other girls laughed.

"I think it would be wonderful, but how can we do it? We're only maids," whined Eva.

"Of course, we can do it," said Miriam.

But could they really do it? Miriam turned the problem over in her mind. She looked at her friends, sitting laughing on the concrete football pitch. They had no costumes, no musicians. They only knew a few rudimentary dances that Miriam remembered from her days working in the tourist hotel.

"Have you decided what dance you plan to do at the festival? The Consulate needs to get the program to the printer," said Dina, speaking over the phone. Miriam was lying on her bunk in her cabin.

"I'm still not sure. Most of the girls want to do the monkey dance, but I don't know where we would get the chorus. Until we decide on that we can't really get the costumes, and . . ."

Miriam's voiced trailed off. *Aiiiyyaaaa!* it was only one month to go, the girls needed to rehearse, and . . .

"I was thinking maybe you could do the *Ramayana*. You don't need a chorus, just some guy to play Prince Rama," said Dina.

"Where am I going to find somebody to play the prince?"

There was a long pause on the other end of the phone. Then Miriam remembered, "I think Leila has a boyfriend. Maybe he could do it."

"I've called the Consulate and they said we can use the auditorium for rehearsals," said Dina, changing the subject. "But you need to make up your mind soon about the dance. We need to get started." Miriam snapped her mobile phone closed, thought a few moments, then called Leila.

It was the first day of rehearsal. They had arranged to use the auditorium of the Consulate, and they were waiting for the church service to end, so they could take the stage.

"Where is Eva?" Miriam asked impatiently, as the last of the churchgoers filtered out of the hall.

"I think she had to work this Sunday. Her employer is going out of town tomorrow, or something," said Siti. Miriam groaned. What if that happened during a performance?

She turned to Leila, "And where is Ahmed? You promised he would be here on time."

At that moment, Ahmed walked into the auditorium, wearing his black leather jacket and looking a little sheepish. "Sorry,

I'm late. I had some trouble getting away from the hotel." He took off his leather jacket and laid it down on a folding chair. The girls clustered around Ahmed. "Oh, your *pakde* is very handsome," gushed Zuhriah to Leila in Indonesian.

Miriam tried to get the women in line to begin the rehearsal. Besides the members of the Balinese Dance Society, Dina had arranged for six more Indonesian students from the university to round out the cast. She placed Ahmed in the middle. He didn't really have to dance, just look imposing. Zuhriah, who was to play the role of the faithful wife, Princess Sita, stayed close to Ahmed. The rest of the troupe lined up along the stage, ready to begin. They were dressed in their normal street clothes. The costumes, which the Consulate had promised to provide, had not yet arrived.

"If she doesn't take Zuhriah out of the dance, I'm going to quit, and I'll make sure that Ahmed doesn't take part either," said Leila. She cradled the mobile phone to her ear while ironing clothes in her employer's house, stabbing the shirts aggressively in her anger.

"What are you talking about?" Dina was sitting in her usual place in Victoria Park. It was only two weeks before the performance. She had a stack of flyers, advertising the show, beside her. She handed them to the Indonesian women who passed through the park.

"I know what she's doing," continued Leila, before Dina could say anything else. "I can see how she always plays up to Ahmed, how she strokes his arm. She's always looking at him, always asking, 'how am I doing, Ahmeeeed?'" she said drawing out Ahmed's name.

"She's supposed to look at him. She's the princess," said Dina. "What does Ahmed do?"

"He just grins. I can tell he likes the attention . . . and he likes her. And I know she is free in the evenings. Maybe they are already seeing each other."

"But you know Miriam can't pull Zuhriah out of the dance now. It's only two weeks away."

"I don't care." Leila snapped the phone shut without another word. Dina was left staring at her mobile.

"Maybe it was a mistake to let Zuhriah play Princess Sita," said Dina the next day, after Miriam's ship had returned to port.

"What could I do?" answered Miriam, plaintively. "Zuhriah wanted the part and she's the prettiest . . . and anyway, all of the girls like Ahmed."

On the day of the last rehearsal, both Ahmed and Zuhriah were late. It wasn't unusual for Ahmed to be late, since he had to come all the way from Kowloon. But Zuhriah lived and worked on Hong Kong Island. Miriam tried to ignore Leila and focus on the other girls. The costumes had arrived from Indonesia, and the women were happily pulling bright sarongs and elaborate headdresses out of the boxes.

"Oh, how pretty," exclaimed Eva as she held a bright green silk sarong in front of her. Dwi pulled out one of the headdresses and put it on her head. Only Leila ignored the activity. She kept a wary, worried eye on the door.

Finally, Zuhriah rushed in. She tossed her jacket on one of the folding chairs and breathlessly apologized for being late. "My employer kept me ...oh, look, the costumes have arrived." She joined the other girls in admiring the garments. A few minutes later, Ahmed strode into the auditorium, waved at Leila, who frowned back, and he too began to rummage through the boxes.

Leila just stared at the two, and then she abruptly turned and stomped out of the room. Everybody looked at her. "Leila, where are you going? Come back, we need to get started," shouted Miriam.

"What's wrong with her?" asked Eva.

"Oh, be quiet, Eva," said Dina. "Miriam, you stay here and get the rehearsal started. I'll talk to Leila." And Dina walked out of the auditorium.

She found Leila sitting in the Consulate foyer, crying. Dina sat down beside her and put her arm around her.

"Don't be so jealous," Dina said soothingly. "You know that Zuhriah is just a flirt. I'm sure there is nothing going on between them."

"I know he's seeing her," Leila said, between small sobs. "Why else did they come in together?"

Dina didn't try to remind Leila that they actually came in separately. Instead, she took another tack. "Come on back to the rehearsal. You know that Miriam needs everybody today. It is the last time before the performance next week."

Leila sat silently for a few moments. She took the tissue that Dina offered her and dried her eyes. Then she slowly rose to her feet and silently walked back toward the auditorium.

"Zuhriah's going back to Indonesia! What am I going to do?" wailed Miriam a few days later.

"I know. I arranged for her ticket. She's leaving in two days. One of her children got sick, and her husband insisted that she come home right away," said Dina.

"But what are we going to do? There are only four days before the performance. How can we put on the Ramayana without someone to be Princess Sita?"

"Somebody else will just have to take her place."

"But who . . . ?"

Dina was applying makeup in the crowded backstage area of Queen Elizabeth Stadium. The day of the Asian Arts Festival had arrived, and they were due to go on stage in twenty minutes, just after the Japanese *koto* players. Everyone was wearing costumes.

Dina painted Dwi's lips a bright crimson, her eyebrows a dark black. She had shiny fake jewels on either side of her nostrils. Dina pulled her hair into a bun and carefully placed the elaborate headdress on her head. When she was finished, Dwi placed the palms of her hands together – the long artificial nails glistening bright red – and bowed. Dina laughed and moved on to the next dancer.

The performance was running late. It was nearly 4 p.m. when the Japanese women strummed their last notes and the curtain fell. The ladies swished off the stage in their kimonos, brushing past the Balinese Dance Society troupe as they moved nervously toward the stage. Men lifted the instruments from the floor and carried them off stage, other stage men brought out some tree twigs to suggest a forest of ancient India.

Dina hurried out of a side door, half bent over, and found her seat in the front row. A moment later Miriam sat down beside her. The curtain rose. The sound system screeched and then settled down to play the music of the Gamelan. The Balinese Dancers filed out onto the stage, their hands tracing graceful arcs to the music. Behind them came Ahmed, resplendent in a gorgeous headdress, and with a gleaming, bare, chest. And behind him . . . Leila, gloriously decked out in a crimson sarong. The prince's faithful wife, Sita.

Miriam watched nervously, but relaxed as Leila moved confidently into her role. Dina looked over to her and smiled. She whispered, "After all, it's a wife's karma to be at her husband's side."

10.

BULE, BULE

Wiji briskly climbed the stairs that led into the Makati disco. It was early, and the disco was not especially crowded. A few Filipina women were dancing by themselves in the middle of the floor. Two Western expatriates sat around the corner of the bar, nursing schooners of beer, talking among themselves and occasionally looking over at the Filipina women dancing, although they did not make any move to join them. Wiji looked around to see if she recognized anyone. She was supposed to meet Yuni and her new boyfriend later, but she had not shown up yet. She wasn't feeling very friendly that night. As far as she could tell, there were no other Indonesian women in the disco, at least none that she recognized. She sat down at the bar and one of the bartenders handed her a complimentary glass of orange juice. Wiji was well known in the disco, and attracted men willing to spend, so she was popular with the management.

She was alone, which was unusual, since she was a pretty young woman, and the men who prowled the disco looked on her with undisguised interest. But she already had a new beau, if that word could be used to describe William, a 45-year-old construction engineer, already going bald. He lived in Britain but made frequent trips to Hong Kong to work on the new airport. He was due to return in five days. Wiji still saw her Canadian boyfriend Stephen from time-to-time, but his visits to Hong Kong had become less and less frequent. One of the Western men at the far end of the bar turned his head in Wiji's direction and stared at her, but she ignored him. The fact that neither William nor Stephen were in Hong Kong at the moment might not have deterred Wiji from a little adventure, but this evening she just wasn't in the mood, and anyway, she was waiting for her friend.

About a half-hour later Yuni entered the disco, her friend in tow. They quickly spotted Wiji, bathed in the pool of light over the bar, Yuni climbed on a neighboring stool, her boyfriend dragged another stool over to her and sat down. He ordered drinks, a Coca Cola for Yuni, and a pint of San Miguel for himself. He asked Wiji if she wanted something to drink too. Wiji pointed to her orange juice glass, still only half empty, and shook her head.

"This is Bill," said Yuni proudly, gripping one of his hands firmly in her own, as if she was afraid he might run away and chase some of the Filipinas on the dance floor. Wiji nodded her head in a greeting. The two of them sitting together made her feel lonely for William. Her eyes drifted toward the dance floor, her mind, to a time two weeks before. She still remembered the two of them dancing slowly together. It had been late, and the band had finally changed from the raucous disco dance music to slower rhythms. She had draped her arms around William's neck; he had placed his arms around her waist and then slowly massaged the small of her back. When she took him to the airport to leave for the U.K. he had cried.

"You been in Hong Kong long?" the question snapped her out of her reverie. For the first time she looked squarely at Bill. She saw a round, ruddy face with reddish hair. *Bule,* she thought to herself, using the Indonesian word for white person. It seemed especially appropriate for Yuni's boyfriend, since it translated roughly as "piggy." She almost laughed out loud. "About five years," she replied. That seemed to exhaust Bill's conversation, and he lapsed into silence. Wiji and Yuni continued talking in Indonesian.

"Where's your *pakde* tonight *mbak*?" Yuni asked.

"He's coming back here next week . . . tell me about your new boyfriend," she added.

That was all the encouragement Yuni needed to launch into a long story. Bill, it seemed, was from Australia, somewhere in Queensland. "That's in northern Australia where they have the Great Barrier Reef, but I think he lives somewhere inland." Wiji knew where Queensland was. In fact, she had actually been to the Gold Coast on a vacation with Trevor. As Yuni prattled on, her mind again went back to the trip. How Trevor was afraid to go out into the surf for fear of jellyfish, but Wiji had run heedlessly into the water, laughing and splashing, and taunting Trevor to follow her.

"Did you hear that Yuni is getting married?" Wiji was sitting on a bench in Victoria Park, next to Dina. It was Wiji's day off and William would not arrive in Hong Kong until the following day. At first, Wiji was a little confused. "Who is she going to marry?"

"That Australian guy, you know, I think his name is Bill," Dina said.

Wiji was surprised. "How can they be getting married? They only met a few weeks ago. I saw them last weekend at the disco, and they didn't say anything about it."

"Well, she called me the other day," continued Dina. "She wanted to know what twenty thousand Australian dollars was in Hong Kong money. Apparently that's how much Bill earns."

"How much *is* twenty thousand Australian dollars in Hong Kong dollars?" Wiji inquired, suddenly rather curious.

She told her.

"Is that how much he earns a month?" Wiji was impressed.

"No, apparently that's his yearly salary."

"Oh, that's not very much," said Wiji. She did a quick calculation in her head. It wasn't all that much more than what she earned working as a domestic helper in Hong Kong.

"I think he has some kind of job on a farm back in Australia." said Dina.

"Sounds like he is just a *petani misken*. Why does she want to marry him?"

"Well, you know he *is* a *bule*," Dina said. "I guess she feels she might have a better life in Australia. She doesn't want to be a maid for the rest of her life."

Bule, bule. Wiji thought about all of the Western men she had known since coming to Hong Kong. There was Stephen, of course. When he was here, they dined and slept together at the luxury hotel where he stayed. Then there was Trevor, an Englishman. He had taken her on that wonderful vacation to the Gold Coast . . . Now there was William. Who knew what delights awaited from that relationship. In her experience *bule* were businessmen with money – money they were happy to spend on Wiji. They had taken her to dinners and movies and bought her new clothes. Stephen had helped her buy her rice land back in Indonesia. But none had ever talked about marrying her, and that grated.

"It's just unfair!" Wiji suddenly exclaimed.

"What's unfair?"

"Why should Yuni be the one to get married? She's not very pretty or sexy."

Dina said nothing.

Wiji stewed about it for the rest of the afternoon. In her previous relationships, she had never thought about getting married. Indeed, a couple of her boyfriends were already married, and she wasn't sure about William. But Yuni had got her thinking. She was already 26. She was getting a little old to find a husband in Indonesia, even if she was a landowner. Why had none of her boyfriends asked to marry her?

At the airport Wiji waited for William to emerge into the arrival hall. She waved as the sliding doors parted and he walked down the ramp, pushing his luggage cart. She leaned across the rail to give him a kiss on the cheek, and then followed him to the taxi stand, where they drove off toward William's hotel.

A couple hours later they were lying on the spacious bed, exhausted from several rounds of love-making that had commenced almost as soon as they had entered the room and sent the hotel porter away.

"William," she ventured. He turned his face toward her. "Have you thought of making a commitment to me?"

"What do you mean by a commitment?" he asked, warily.

"Well, you know . . . " Wiji groped for words. This kind of conversation was unfamiliar to her. ". . . a commitment, like marriage." There, the word was out.

"Hold on," William said, suddenly becoming more awake. "Aren't you rushing things a little. We haven't known each other very long."

"Well, I have a friend named Yuni . . ." she ventured. Then she stopped.

"Yuni?"

"Never mind," she said and snuggled up closer to him.

During the next two weeks Wiji was careful not to bring the subject up again, and, of course, William didn't say anything about it either. Instead, he prattled on about how they would take a vacation together in Phuket, the next time he came out to Hong Kong. She spent almost every night in William's luxury hotel room, slipping away early in the morning, while William was sleeping, to make breakfast in the home of the expatriate couple where she worked. In the evenings William took her to expensive restaurants. Afterwards, they would go to a movie or spend the evening at a disco. When it came time for William to return to the U.K., Wiji went with him to the airport. "The next time I come out we'll go to Thailand," he said. "Don't forget."

A week later, Wiji was sitting in the disco with Retno. "I heard that Yuni has already gone back to Indonesia," Retno said.

"You mean she has quit her job?" The question sounded foolish as soon as Wiji spoke it. Of course Yuni had quit her job; she was getting married. But Wiji was, by nature, a rather practical young woman, and it shocked her that Yuni would leave her job so easily. But then, she was still surprised that Yuni had agreed to marry a man she had met in a disco only one week previously.

"Her sister told me that she's working in a bar in Jakarta, waiting for Bill to get her a visa so she can go to Australia and get married."

"She didn't go back to her home town?"

"No, the family isn't very happy with the idea of her marrying a foreigner, not to mention a Christian."

Wiji thought about that for a few moments. She could imagine the reaction in her own family if she brought home a Western boyfriend and announced that she was getting married. She had never taken any of her boyfriends back to her town, even though some of them had pressed her to do so. She thought for a moment about introducing William to her family then pushed the thought out of her mind.

"Why do you think Yuni would go to so much trouble to marry a Western guy and just cause trouble with her family?" Wiji asked.

"Maybe she just saw her chance and grabbed it. I mean, look at the odds against us here. There must be more than 40,000 of us in Hong Kong now, and maybe three times that many Filipinas. How many Indonesian men are here? Maybe a few sailors?"

"What kind of men are you going to meet in a place like this?" she said, waving an arm at the bar, where several middle-aged Western men were nursing drinks. "The older guys are usually married, and the young single men just want to have fun with you. There are too many single women here; they're spoiled."

Back in Indonesia, Wiji's mother had been thinking about Wiji's future too. Most of the young women in their small town got married when they were twenty or younger. Wiji was already getting to be something of an old maid. And, of course, her living and working in Hong Kong complicated matters. But Wiji's mother was not deterred by these obstacles. For one thing, Wiji was a landowner. She had already bought a hectare of rice land from her savings as a domestic helper, and that rice land brought in an income of nearly two million rupiah every month, certainly an attractive inducement for any young man. And, of course, Wiji was still very pretty, even if she was getting old. She started making inquiries, showing a picture of Wiji she had sent to her from Hong Kong.

There was a young man in the small town named Jurur, who looked like a good prospect. He was a little younger than Wiji and held a post in the town administration. He was good-looking in a quiet sort of way, and very conscientious. Wiji's mother considered him a very suitable match and showed him her daughter's picture and promised to introduce him when Wiji came back home.

"There is somebody I want you to meet," her mother told Wiji when, a couple of months later, Wiji had returned to her hometown for a short visit after spending a long weekend in Bali with William. She had persuaded him to change his holiday from Phuket, so that she could visit her home. He flew back to Hong Kong and then to Britain, while Wiji had flown to Surabaya and then taken a bus to her home. She brought presents with her: a jade pendant for her mother; a couple of rings for her sisters. William had helped buy them for her in Hong Kong. "Who do you want me to meet?" Wiji said warily.

"Wiji . . ." Her mother had rehearsed this set piece ever since she learned that Wiji would be returning for a visit. ". . . it is time that you came home and got married. You've been working in Hong Kong now for five years. You are already 26. All of your sisters are married, and some of them have children. You have been able to buy a rice field from your savings, so there are many men who would find you to be a good wife, even if you are getting old. It is not so good for you to live alone in Hong Kong."

The meeting with Jurur took place the next day. He arrived wearing a bright new batik shirt and carried a present of sweet meats. Wiji wore a pale blue sarong. Her mother had tied her hair in a black, glistening bun. She did most of the talking, directing her polite questions to Jurur, who replied with equally polite phrases, thanking her for the tea and fried banana cake. From time to time, he looked over at Wiji but didn't talk to her directly very much. "Living in Hong Kong must be very exciting," he said once. Wiji just nodded politely. The conversation went on in this vein until Jurur excused himself, and Wiji and her mother saw him away at the door.

"Jurur is willing to marry you," Wiji's mother explained patiently the next day.

"He's only interested in my rice field," Wiji countered. Inwardly, she bridled at the implication that she had to be grateful that some low-level clerk in this small town would stoop to marry her, a mere maid. At her mother's insistence, she had gone walking with Jurur, but they had little to say to each other. Jurur had scarcely been out of the town except to attend university. He asked what she did in her free time, and she replied that she met her friends in Victoria Park. He asked if he could write to her in Hong Kong, and she said yes.

True to his word, Jurur wrote Wiji letters regularly from Indonesia. They seemed stilted compared with the e-mails she still received occasionally from Stephen, and the ardent, long-distance phone calls she got from William, almost every day. She tried to imagine life in her small town with Jurur. Probably he would make her stay at home and wear a head scarf whenever she went out of the house. He would take over managing her rice land and spend most of his time sitting around talking with his friends, while she stayed in the house with her sisters.

Climbing the steps into the disco, Wiji spotted Retno sitting in the corner booth and she sidled next to her. The waitress brought her a complimentary orange juice. "I heard that Yuni is in Australia now. They finally got married," said Retno. "Yes," said Wiji, "I got an e-mail from her the other day." At the end of the bar a rather handsome middle-aged *bule* stared at Wiji. She smiled back at him.

"What's happening between you and William?"

"He's coming back to Hong Kong in a couple of weeks. This time he says he'll definitely take me to Phuket."

11.

Please Don't Leave Me

He was easy to spot, walking briskly down Sugar Street toward Victoria Park, being about a head taller than most of the Chinese people who filled the busy street. Dina had first noticed him earlier in the week, when he entered the park from the same route and stopped briefly to chat with Wati and her friends. He had smiled in her direction. Dina just smiled shyly in return, but said nothing. Then the man had waved goodbye, walked into the park, and disappeared.

It seemed to Dina that he appeared about the same time every day – in the late afternoon – and she wondered what he was doing at this time of day. Did he work in one of the nearby office towers? Dina was grateful to have something to occupy her mind, since she was feeling bored, as she often did late in the afternoon on a slow weekday. Today she was feeling drowsy since she had been up late the previous night. She had taken the subway to Kowloon to buy more rupiah from a woman who supplied her with bank notes to trade. She had barely been able to catch the last subway back to Causeway Bay before it closed down for the night.

The sight of the young man approaching the park again snapped her out of her torpor. As he waited by the curb for the light to change she studied him carefully. He was a *bule*, a Westerner, and seemed to her to be in his mid-thirties, about her own age. He dressed casually, with an open shirt and sport coat, but no tie. He had black, rather curly hair. At this distance she could not make out the color of his eyes. She thought they were brown. At that moment the light changed and the stranger strode across the street.

Normally, Dina didn't talk much with Wati, even though they spent many hours together. Wati loved to gossip, and Dina didn't like to have all of her affairs spread around the park – not that she provided much grist for the gossip mill. But this time her curiosity over the stranger got the better of her, and she casually inquired about the man.

"I think he is British," Wati replied. "Why? Do you want a boyfriend?"

Dina shook her head and said nothing more. She knew it was a mistake to talk to Wati.

That evening Dina looked at herself for a long time in the mirror that she used for cutting hair. Though she was adept at styling other women's hair, she couldn't help but notice that she had not paid much attention to her own. It just kind of fell down on either side of her head. She ran a comb through her hair letting the strands fall over her forehead, trying to imagine herself with a shorter cut and possibly bangs down her forehead. She pulled a pair of scissors out of the drawer and began hacking away. Clumps of black hair fell to the floor at her feet. After a few minutes, she looked again appraisingly at the image of herself in the mirror. "Yes, that looks better," she thought.

Next she began to rummage though her clothes closet. It was mostly stuffed with jeans, nondescript blouses, and sweaters – the ordinary wardrobe that she wore most days in the park. At the bottom of the wardrobe she found what she was looking for, a shoe box with a pair of smart-looking sandals inside. She had bought them a few months previously but never worn them. She pulled them out of the box, shucked off her sneakers and inserted her toes through the straps, holding them out in front of her to admire. They made her feel prettier. Then she placed them back in the box, pulled on the old T-shirt that she used as a nightshirt, and climbed into her narrow bed.

The next morning Dina took a little longer with her makeup. She also took more care in selecting her clothes. Maybe she should go shopping at one of the Japanese department stores tonight, she thought. She finally settled on a pair of beige pants and a pale-blue blouse, which went nicely with her new sandals. She took another look at her image in the mirror, pulled out her scissors, and made a few repairs. Then she gathered her magazines, put them in her carry-on case and left her apartment to go to Victoria Park.

The hours seemed to drag. Dina sold a few magazines and phonecards. One of her regular customers stopped by to exchange a thousand dollars for rupiah, and lingered a while. "You've cut your hair, *mbak*? It looks nice." Dina thanked her for the compliment but kept an eye on Sugar Street. A few moments later the woman got up from the concrete bench and waved goodbye. Dina looked at her watch. It was already past 3 p.m. When did he usually come by? She hung around the park late, well past 6 p.m., but it was obvious that he was not going to pass through the park that day.

The next day was Saturday, and Dina was busy. Indonesian Independence Day was approaching, and the park was full of maids needing to send some money back to their home or to buy phonecards to call home on the holiday. Around 6 p.m. she packed the unsold magazines and walked back to her apartment. There she merely dumped her stuff before heading out again. She crossed Hennessy Road and entered the Mitsukoshi Department Store, where she spent an hour browsing among the racks of dresses and pants. She picked out a red halter, purchased it and stuffed it into her handbag. Then she exited the department store and walked over to check out the Esprit store.

Before she got to the entrance, however, she spotted the stranger striding down the sidewalk. Panic seized her. She was about to duck into the store, when the man spotted her.

"Hi," he said as he strode up. "You're one of the women in the park, aren't you?"

Dina felt trapped and embarrassed, although she didn't quite know why. His sudden appearance had thrown her off balance. What was he doing here anyway? Finally she broke her silence.

"Yes, I remember seeing you . . . you didn't come by the park yesterday . . ."

"Oh, that was my day off. What are you doing?"

Dina told him that she was just out shopping. "I was going in here," she said, pointing to the fashionable shop.

"Well, I don't want to keep you. See you in the park," he said. Then he pulled out his wallet and extracted a business card and handed it to Dina, waved goodbye and sauntered down the sidewalk.

Dina placed the card in her purse and entered the store. She wandered aimlessly among the clothing racks then left the store without buying anything. She walked back to her apartment and lay down on the bed, staring at the ceiling for a few moments. Then she picked up her purse and took out the card, turning it over with her fingers. The words on the card read:

Nicholas Last
Trainer

And it listed the name of the fitness club where he worked in Causeway Bay. Dina remembered that it was next to the Esprit store. She stared some more at the ceiling before dozing off.

Sunday was busy, and she put Nick out of her mind. But on Monday she left the park early and walked over to the

Mitsukoshi store. This time she passed by the racks of dresses and street clothes and headed for the athletic department, where she purchased a sweatshirt and pants, a pair of athletic shorts and some new tennis shoes. She put them in the small carry-on case she had brought with her. Then she walked over to the fitness center.

"We have a full year membership for five hundred dollars a month," the Chinese salesman told her.

"I was thinking of something more like a month," Dina countered.

The salesman put on a grave face and tried to explain the savings that she would enjoy through a full membership – "and we have a discount on . . . and you will have full use of all the facilities . . ." They finally settled on a two-month membership.

"Your trainer will be Vincent Tse . . ."

"Oh, I was expecting to choose my own trainer. See . . . I have this . . ." She pulled out the business card and showed it to the salesman.

"Ah, Nick. I think he is already booked. Now I'll arrange a session with Vincent."

Dina said nothing more. The Chinese man got up and returned with her membership card. She put it in her handbag, grabbed her carry-on case, and got up. She took the escalator down to the changing room and put on her new athletic clothes, placing her street clothes in the locker. She paused a few moments before the mirror, hoping that her new outfit looked smart. Then she ascended the stairs to the vast exercise room.

She picked out a treadmill and spent a few moments trying to figure out how the mechanism worked. The salesman had told her that her trainer would help her, but she said that she preferred to work out by herself. She finally turned the machine on to a slow pace and started walking. She surveyed the room, filled with Chinese, puffing away on the other treadmills, or working a bewildering array of other mechanical devices in the distance. Once she thought she spotted Nick but it turned out to be another Western man.

A few minutes later, while Dina was slowly chugging away, staring blankly at the television monitors arrayed in front of her, she felt a tap on her shoulder.

"I thought I recognized you," Nick said. "I didn't know that you came here. I don't remember seeing you before."

"I just joined." Dina smiled. "I thought that you would be my trainer, but that salesman said you were already booked."

She was still slowly pacing along the treadmill, Nick reached over and turned it off. "I think maybe I can work you in."

For the next hour, Nick guided her through the complexities of the rowing machines, the ab pressers, the inversion table. Dina was sweating, but pleasantly tired and tingling with pleasure by the time the session ended and Nick told her he had leave to help another customer. She grabbed her towel and descended to the basement changing room. She had written her mobile phone number on one of Nick's business cards and given it back to him before she left.

Dina went to the fitness center every afternoon. Sometimes Nick helped her navigate the fitness jungle. If he was busy, she occupied her time on the treadmill. She did not use the services of any other trainer. During the day he called Dina on her mobile phone. Dina would turn her head away from Wati and whisper back. In the evening they sometimes dined together at a small Thai restaurant near the fitness center. Dina wanted to take him to one of her favorite Indonesian restaurants in Causeway Bay, but she was afraid they might be seen together and gossiped about in the park.

With Nick, Dina opened up as she had never done with anyone else, certainly nobody in the park. She told him how she had come to Hong Kong ten years before to work as a domestic helper, and how she had developed her numerous small businesses. She told him about her home in Indonesia, where her brother still lived, working as a school teacher. She proudly mentioned that she had purchased several rice fields with her earnings.

Nick told her how he had come to Hong Kong from Sydney in the last giddy year before the handover to China, when it was still possible for expatriates from Commonwealth countries to work in Hong Kong without having to get visas. "I wanted to see Hong Kong the way it was, before it was changed forever," he said. For a while he had worked as a bartender in a pub in Central that catered to British businessmen. Then he had found the job at the fitness center. That night they went back to his apartment on the far side of Victoria Park. While making love, she whispered, "please don't leave me."

She usually awoke long before Nick, slipping out of his bed and quietly putting on her clothes. She rode the elevator down to the street and took a taxi back to her own place, where she showered, changed into fresh clothes, gathered her magazines and other things, then went out for another day's work in the park.

In the afternoon Nick walked down Sugar Street in his usual loping gait and crossed over to the park. He stopped for a few moments to banter with Wati. Then he smiled over at Dina and walked on through the park. Dina had asked Nick not to pay her too much attention when he walked across the park to his place in the late afternoon, and he had reluctantly agreed.

"He's nice for a British guy," Wati remarked to Dina after Nick had disappeared in the crowd.

"Australian. He's an Australian," Dina corrected her.

"Oh? How do you know that?"

"Well . . . you can tell by his accent . . ."

Dina knew that she had made a mistake. Wati said nothing but gave her a knowing smile.

But it was obvious that Wati had begun to pay closer attention to Dina's movements. She often commented on them, and made remarks about the changes in her appearance.

"What do you do when you leave the park so early?" she inquired one afternoon.

"Oh, I just go over to Nurma's Place," Dina replied. Wati and Nurma didn't get along, so that was a safe excuse.

"That's a nice new sweater you have. Who bought it for you?" Wati asked the next day.

"Nobody. I bought it myself." Actually, Nick had bought it for her when they were strolling together through the mall next to the fitness center.

"Retno says she saw you with some guy at a restaurant in Wanchai last night. Got a new boyfriend?" asked Wati.

"Retno talks a lot of rubbish," Dina replied.

Dina moved to a new place on a bench inside the park. "I'm tired of listening to Wati all day," she told Nurma, who had come out of her place to get a little fresh air. A few minutes later, Nick entered the park on his way home. He waved discreetly to Dina but didn't stop to talk. "Is that him?" Nurma nudged Dina. "Your *pakde* is very handsome."

"Don't say anything to the girls at your place," Dina pleaded. Nurma nodded and smiled. Then she got up and walked out of the park.

A few days later, Retno sat down beside her. Dina did not particularly like Retno, who was a close buddy of Wati. Dina said nothing, hoping that Retno would leave. But she was in a talkative mood.

"Wanchai is getting too crowded. I only made a hundred last night."

"Maybe you should get yourself a boyfriend, like Wiji," Dina responded.

"It's not so easy, you know. I had this American guy, but he went home. But I hear you have a new boyfriend."

Before she could reply, Nick entered the park on his way home. Silently Dina prayed that he would not pay any attention to her, but he gave a brief wave, and Retno waved back.

The next night Dina was alone in her apartment. Nick had said he was having dinner with some of his mates and that he would be late. "Don't worry," Dina had said. "I have to get ready for tomorrow." Tomorrow was Sunday, her busiest day, and she had to collect all of the things she would try to sell.

Her mobile phone burred, and Dina flipped it open, thinking it might be Nick. But the number on the display wasn't his.

"This is Retno. I'm here in the Big Apple, and I can see your *pakde* having a good time." Dina could barely make out the words against the background of loud disco music. She snapped her phone shut and lay back on her bed. She thought about going to Wanchai and looking herself, but decided not to. She punched Nick's number into her phone.

"The number you have called is unavailable at the moment. Please try again later."

Later Dina confronted Nick in his apartment.

"What were you doing in Wanchai last night?" she said.

"What do you mean? I wasn't in Wanchai," Nick replied.

"My friend saw you last night at the Big Apple. Don't deny it, I know. I have a lot of friends who go to Wanchai."

"I went there with some of my mates after we had dinner. What's wrong with that? Why shouldn't I . . ." At that moment his mobile phone burred. He flipped it open, listened a few moments, then said, "I'll call you back later."

"Who was that?" Dina cried as he snapped his phone shut.

"Just a friend . . ."

After that Dina stormed out of Nick's apartment and walked in the dark across Victoria Park to her own place.

The next day she did not go to the fitness center as usual. Retno came over and sat down beside her on the bench. Dina didn't want to talk, but something made her open up. "Nick told me he just went to the Big Apple with some of his friends," she said, forgetting that she had denied knowing Nick before.

Retno laughed. "He was there most of the night. I think I saw him with one of the Filipina PR girls sitting on his lap. You know you can't trust *bule*. They just want to use you and leave you. They've got girlfriends all over."

Dina was plunged into gloom. The worst thing about it was that her story was probably all over the park. By now everybody knew that Dina's boyfriend was just playing with her. She resolved that she should stop seeing Nick, stop going to the fitness center. A few minutes later her mobile phone buzzed. She saw on the display that it was Nick's number, and she snapped it closed. Five minutes later the phone rang again. This time she answered, but hearing Nick's voice, she closed her phone again without saying anything. That evening she wandered aimlessly around Causeway Bay. Why, she asked herself, should anyone like Nick be interested in her anyway? After all, she was just a kind of street hawker. Retno was right. All *bule* wanted was to play games with girls and then leave them. A couple times her phone rang. But they were customers calling, and not Nick.

For the next several days, Nick failed to show up in the park. Nor did he call. Several times Dina grabbed her mobile out of her purse, thinking it might be Nick calling, but all of the calls were from women wanting to buy phonecards.

She had already moved back to her regular place at the entrance to Victoria Park, sitting next to Wati and the other regulars, when she saw him in the distance, walking down Sugar Street. Suddenly she felt her body tense. What would she do if he came up to her? She decided that she would ignore him. Let him talk to Wati. But after crossing the street, he headed straight for her and sat down next to her. He didn't say anything but pulled out an envelope with a single word, *Dina*, written on the front. He took her purse, opened it, and put the envelope inside. Then he got up and walked away without saying a word.

As soon as she got home, she opened the envelope. Inside was a card with a picture of a red rose on the front. She could read his own handwriting at the bottom: "I'm sorry," and at the bottom, "I love you. Nick." That night he called her on her mobile phone.

"Hi, what are you doing?"

"Nothing." Dina replied. And then, after a pause, she said, "thank you for your card."

They talked some more. In spite of herself, Dina found herself warming to his voice.

Then Nick said, "Can I ask you something?"

"Yes," she replied cautiously.

"Why don't you want me to stop and talk with you in the park. Why do you want to meet in out-of-the-way places? Are you embarrassed to be seen with me?"

"No!" Dina exclaimed. "I'm just afraid people will talk about us . . ."

"So what if they do?"

Dina didn't reply. How could she explain what she really feared – her deep-seated fear that Nick would leave her, and everybody in the park would know about it. Everybody would talk about it for days and tell her she was a fool, and why would any foreigner love a woman like her . . . She didn't think she could stand it.

The next day Nick walked directly over to where Dina was sitting. He sat down beside her, Dina sliding down a little to make room. He nodded at Wati. Then he smiled at Dina and they began talking. When he got up to go, Nick planted a kiss, which Dina warmly received. She looked over at Wati and Retno and smiled. That night Dina returned to Nick's apartment. While they were making love, she whispered in his ear again, "Please don't leave me."

12.

A Night in TST

The gangplank fell with a resounding clank, and Retno rose from the bench and joined the people scrambling off the ferry. She crossed onto the quay and walked through the exit into Tsim Sha Tsui, passing a crowd of expatriates emerging from the Cultural Center after a performance, chatting as they walked toward the ferry for the ride back to Hong Kong island. Along the waterfront, many Chinese couples still sat on the concrete seats, holding hands and looking across the harbor at the lights of the city. Overhead the steeple clock tower showed a few minutes before eleven. Soon the Star Ferry would shut down for the evening, and Retno would be stranded on Kowloon side, unless she was willing to pay the subway charge to get back to Hong Kong. A taxi was out of the question.

Retno felt more comfortable on the Hong Kong side of the harbor, where she spent her days in Victoria Park and her evenings in Wanchai, or at the boarding houses of her friends. She had crossed over to Kowloon, hoping to meet her ex-boyfriend, Ahmed. "I'll meet you in front of the clock tower," he had said reluctantly when she had called him on her mobile phone earlier in the day. When she saw that he wasn't standing next to the clock tower, Retno punched in Ahmed's number again, but got only a recorded message: *The number you have called is unavailable at the moment. Please try again later.* "Maybe he's still working," she thought.

Ahmed was a doorman at a luxury hotel. They had met during a brief time that Retno worked as a charwoman at the same hotel. She took the job shortly after she was terminated as a domestic helper. She liked working at the hotel, and sometimes she could find a place to sleep in one of the vacant rooms. But she quit after the hotel management failed to pay her wages, and, being an overstay, there wasn't much she could do about it.

As she walked along the esplanade, Retno spotted Sussy, talking with two young South Asian men. As Retno approached, the young men smiled at Sussy and walked away. Sussy seemed unperturbed at the interruption and greeted Retno in a friendly manner. "What brings you over here?" she asked. "Are you looking for anyone in particular, or are you just cruising?" she said.

"I'm waiting to see Ahmed. He should be here any minute."

"I thought you broke up with Ahmed a long time ago. I sometimes see him and that other girl – what's her name – in Victoria Park."

"Well . . ." Retno really didn't want to go into the story.

"I always thought Ahmed was cute," Sussy continued. "I wondered why you broke up with him. I wouldn't mind going with him."

"He wouldn't give you any money," Retno replied testily.

"I don't care. I'd go with him for free," said Sussy, whose attention was diverted by another passing man. She smiled at him.

Retno had lived in Ahmed's small apartment for nearly six months after she quit working at the hotel. Sometimes they had dinner at one of the Pakistani restaurants in that vast city-within-a-city called Chungking Mansions or they would walk together at night along the esplanade, sitting on the concrete benches and looking out across Victoria Harbor. When Ahmed worked days she often killed time in Victoria Park, gossiping with Wati, a short, dumpy Indonesian woman who changed money.

It was a little past midnight by the hands on the clock tower. The Star Ferry had shut down for the night and so had all of the buses. The subway would run until 1 a.m., so she still could get back to Hong Kong side, if she were willing to spend the eleven dollars for the fare. She was tempted. She looked into her purse and found a hundred-dollar note, a single twenty-dollar note, and enough loose change to pay the subway fare back to Hong Kong island. There, she could spend the rest of the night in one of the Wanchai discos, slouching in one of the back booths, enveloped in the darkness and oblivious to the thunder of the disco music. She put the thought out of her mind. And once more punched Ahmed's number into her mobile phone. Once more she got the recorded voice. "Please try again later."

Retno had been living with Ahmed for about six months when, one Sunday afternoon, while she was in Victoria Park talking with some of her friends, she thought she saw him holding hands with another Indonesian woman. She was a little surprised. She understood that Ahmed had to work on Sunday afternoons – anyway, that was what he told her. He didn't make much of an effort to deny that he had been seeing another. "It's only one day in the week," he had said, with his grin that Retno usually found so winning. This time she said nothing. She simply gathered her few possessions and stuffed them in her carry-on suitcase and walked out. She caught a bus back to Victoria Park. It was late in the summer, and the weather was still hot, so she slept on one of the grassy slopes. In the morning, she bathed in the public shower and stashed her carry-on suitcase in one of the toilet stalls.

The hands on the big clock had now moved past one. The subway had shutdown for the night. Retno was stuck on the Kowloon side – for the next six hours at least – until public transport came alive again. Sussy had already left too, linking her arms in those of a burly Indian man and giving Retno a jaunty wave goodbye. It was beginning to look like Ahmed would not show up. He should have been off duty by now.

Sometimes Wati let her stay at her place, sleeping on the floor of the boarding house that Wati shared with two other women. Both of them, like Retno, were overstays. She spent her days sitting in Victoria Park, occasionally running little errands, like walking over to the 7-Eleven to buy a bottle of water. Sometimes she sold some of Wati's phonecards, while she went to the toilet, or back to her place to take a nap. But most of the time she just sat on the bench, listening to Wati's comments about other Indonesians in the park. Retno liked to gossip, and because of the nights she spent in Wanchai discos, she picked up a lot of information about the after-hours activities of some of their colleagues, which Wati lapped up.

It was already past two, yet there were still people walking along the waterfront, couples hand-in-hand, or snuggling on the concrete benches. Retno suddenly felt a wave of loneliness come over her. It was clear by now that Ahmed was not going to show up. She wished that Sussy were still with her. Sussy should have finished her engagement by now, but maybe she had wheedled enough money out of her client to pay for a taxi ride back to Hong Kong island and her boarding house.

Feeling the hardness of the concrete bench beneath her, she was tempted to pay for a taxi herself, but she reflected that it would take almost all of the money that she had with her, and she was not certain where she would get more. She felt a pang of hunger – it had been hours since she had last eaten – and decided to see if she could find a place still open at this hour.

She stood up and walked into Kowloon, past the gray bulk of the Peninsula Hotel. Even at this hour, people in evening clothes were arriving at the grand front entrance, assisted out of limousines by Chinese doormen, immaculately dressed in white uniforms. For a moment she thought of Ahmed in his doorman's uniform. She walked down Nathan Road, still bright with neon and busy with pedestrians, even at this late hour. She crossed Nathan Road in front of Chungking Mansions. Several Indian prostitutes – resplendent in bright red or green saris – were loitering at the entrance bantering with several Indian men.

Retno wandered through the empty corridors, but all of the stalls were closed, the metal curtains drawn down and secured with large padlocks. Out of the shadows a dark-skinned Indian man wearing a turban emerged. He stared at Retno but said nothing, gliding past her down the hall. Retno shuddered and decided to leave, but got lost trying to find her way through the maze. She turned down one corridor only to come to a dead end. She retreated, and turned down another, only to find her way blocked by a metal grating. A cat meowed from behind it and scurried away. Retno hurried back, panic building, to turn down yet another corridor. At the end she thought she could see the glow of neon. She emerged onto Nathan road, sweating and breathing heavily. The Indian prostitutes were gone.

A few blocks away she spotted a McDonald's that was still open. Compared to Chungking Mansions, it seemed warm and inviting. She remembered that she was hungry and walked in. At the counter a sleepy Chinese attendant served her chicken wings and French fries, took her money and gave her a dollar in change. She took her tray and turned to choose a table in the nearly empty restaurant. In one corner she spotted a woman resting her blond head on her arms on the table. Retno walked past her and set her tray down at the next table. She was startled when the woman raised her head. It was Sussy.

Her eyes were bloodshot from crying, and there was still some dried blood at the corner of her mouth.

"Sussy. What happened?" asked Retno. She picked up one of the paper napkins from her tray and dabbed it against Sussy's mouth. Sussy dropped her head back into her arms. "I don't want to talk about it."

Retno nudged her head and offered her some of her French fries. Sussy lifted her head, stared at the cup of fries, took one of them and put it in her mouth. Then she took another. "I haven't eaten in a while," she said.

The food seemed to revive her spirits slightly, and she began to recount her story. She had left Retno with the Indian man, who had taken her back to his tiny room in the same Chungking Mansions. Sussy had taken his two hundred dollars, taken off her clothes and lain down on the bed. When they had finished and Sussy was starting to put her clothes back on, the man has grabbed her forcefully by the arm, twisting it. Sussy had shouted in pain and tried to strike back with her other hand. But the Indian man was too strong. With his other hand he grabbed her wallet. Then he pushed her out of the door.

"He took everything I have. I don't even have enough to get back home," she said.

"Don't worry. I'll take you back with me," Retno said patting her arm.

"Did you ever meet up with Ahmed?" Sussy asked, changing the subject.

"No. He never showed up."

Sussy didn't say anything. She wasn't surprised.

They sat together in silence. The chicken wings and French fries were gone. Finally Retno nudged her. "It's almost daylight, morning. Maybe we'd better go."

Sussy straightened up and fished in her bag for her compact. She looked at her face in the mirror and grimaced. Then she began dabbing some lipstick on her mouth. She closed the compact, dropped it in her purse and rose from the table.

Light was already beginning to creep down among the office towers as Sussy and Retno left the restaurant, walking hand-in-hand along Nathan Road. On the street, old men flopped bundles of newspapers in front of kiosks and began sorting through them. Street cleaners moved their brooms along the curbs. An old lady slowly navigated a pushcart loaded with plastic garbage bags. As they approached the terminal, the clock tower showed 6:15. The Star Ferry would be running again. Retno dropped coins in the turnstile, and the two walked up the concrete stairs onto the ferry. Already it looked like it was going to be a fine, warm, day. Retno thought about finding a comfortable piece of grass in Victoria Park and curling up to go to sleep for the rest of the day. She knew the spot.

13.

Downsized

Everybody in Hong Kong, it seemed, was being downsized. The Asian financial crisis cut a wide swathe through the expatriate community, and the Crowder family of No. 10A Red Hill Drive had not escaped. The Crowders had moved to Hong Kong five years previously from a large city in the Mid-West, Mr. Crowder sent out to manage the company's East Asia operations. But when the accountants back in the Mid-Western city totaled up the costs of maintaining the Crowders – the subsidies they paid so that the family could live in an expensive row house in a fashionable area overlooking Stanley Bay; the fees required to send the Crowders' two children, Amy and Bruce, to the International School; the membership in the American Club, where Mrs. Crowder often went to play tennis with the wives of other managers and financial analysts – and absorbed these figures and compared them with the declining profits from East Asian sales, they concluded that the whole operation might just as well be run out of Tokyo. Mr. Crowder was informed that the Hong Kong office would be closed in two months.

Mrs. Crowder took the news calmly and turned her attention to the practicalities of moving her family back to the United States. In truth, Mrs. Crowder was not unhappy with the turn of events. She was rather glad to be returning to her home city, even if it meant giving up some of the luxuries she had come to enjoy in Hong Kong. She looked over the living room and began mentally deciding what would be retained, packed, and shipped back to America. What would be sold, and what might simply be left behind for whomever took over their house – expat triage. Of course, she would keep the expensive Persian carpet that covered almost the entire floor. And there was the dark elm-wood cabinet and the silk tapestry of the Eight Chinese Immortals that hung on the living room wall. Her pride was the round, black, cherry-wood dining table. She was already beginning to imagine what it would look like in her new home. How amusing it would be to serve her friends Cantonese dishes on it. Except, as she ruefully reflected, she had neglected to take those Chinese cooking courses. She left the cooking to Theresa.

Theresa walked into her tiny bedroom, closed the door and leaned her back against it. She had just finished talking with Mrs. Crowder, who had informed her that Mr. Crowder had lost his job. "He's being downsized; they're closing the Hong Kong office and moving all of the operations to Tokyo" – is how Mrs. Crowder had put it. She looked around her room. Like all of the maids' rooms on Red Hill Drive, it was small but cozy. There was a pale-yellow comforter on her narrow bed, and the pillows had fringes. To one side was a plastic cabinet with four drawers. They contained most of her possessions: cosmetics; a small wooden box with a few pieces of jewelry that she wore to church on Sundays, when she went to church; a collection of Indonesian love songs on cassette tapes; her underwear and stockings. On the top of the cabinet was a small color television set and on top of that a plastic Hello Kitty doll that Mrs. Crowder had brought back for her from a trip to Japan. On one side of the room was a single shelf, on which sat: a tape cassette player; a plastic figurine of Jesus; and two color photos – one of her husband and the other of their two children, a girl, fourteen and a boy, ten. They were dressed in the white and blue uniform of the convent school they attended in Jakarta. Already she was beginning to make a mental note of what she would do with her things. Mrs. Crowder would probably dispose of the bed and plastic cabinet in an expat sale. She could probably fit most of her clothes and the rest of her possessions in one suitcase and possibly another plastic bag.

That evening Mrs. Crowder and her husband lingered at the round cherry-wood dining table. Dinner was over. The children had gone to the game room to play videos. Theresa cleared the last dishes from the table and took them to the kitchen. She quietly immersed them in water, wanting to keep the noise down so that she could hear snatches of the conversations coming from the other room.

"Should we keep Amy and Bruce in the International School until the end of the term?"

"I don't know. Their education allowance will be cut off in a month or so. I don't know whether we can afford to keep them there until the end of the term."

"I don't like the idea of them leaving school mid-term. And you know that Amy is looking forward to going on the class trip to Paris in the spring."

There was a short pause.

"Have you given any thought to finding another job here in Hong Kong? I hate to disrupt the children when they've settled in so well."

"I plan to talk to Marc next week. There is a possibility there . . . But you know his company is under the same pressures we're feeling."

"I wonder if Amy and Bruce will be able to fit into a public school back in the States, after they've been here so long."

The conversation died. Mr. Crowder got up and went to his study. Mrs. Crowder went into the game room to check on the children. Theresa finished the dishes and went to her room, where she lay on the bed for several hours staring at the ceiling.

The next day, Theresa caught the bus to Causeway Bay. She wanted to buy a phonecard so that she could call her husband in Indonesia and tell him the sad news. She found Dina sitting on a bench near the entrance to Victoria Park. The park was relatively deserted on this week day. Dina was alone, so after she had pocketed the card in her purse, Theresa lingered to talk.

"So, you have Thursday off, *mbak?*" ventured Dina.

"No. I just came down to buy a phonecard to call home. I have to get back soon. My employer doesn't know I left." She hesitated a little. "You see, I think I'm going to be terminated."

"You think?"

"Well, my employers are being downsized," Theresa said.

"Downsized?" Dina seemed puzzled by the expression, which Theresa had spoken in English. She had never heard the word before. She chewed it over in her mind. "Downsized?" That sounds like something that happens to your husband after you have finished making love." They both laughed. Then Theresa turned serious again.

"It means they might have to go back to America."

"I see," said Dina. "So what are you going to do now?"

"I don't know for sure. You see, I have two children in a convent school in Jakarta. Most of my salary goes to pay their fees. If I'm terminated, I guess I'll have to send them back to my village and put them in a government school . . . if they can find room. That's what I have to talk to my husband about."

Both of the women sat in silence for a few moments. A minibus pulled up to the curb and disgorged its passengers. One of them was Indonesian, and Dina shifted her attention to her: "*majalas*, rupiah," she chanted. She turned her attention back to Theresa. "Have you talked with your agency? Maybe they can get you another job here."

"No, not yet. I suppose I'll have to try, but I don't know what chance I'll have. Maybe everybody is being downsized."

Mr. Crowder walked into the American Club coffee shop and found a table. The waiter greeted him with a friendly, "Good morning, Mr. Crowder. Breakfast today?" He looked at the Chinese man and at the shiny brass nameplate on the chest of his immaculate white tunic. "Not today, Gus, I'm meeting somebody. He might like to eat, though." He sat down and looked out of the window. It presented a wide vista of Victoria Harbor and across the water.

Soon Marc arrived, plumped himself down in the opposite chair and picked up a menu. "You're not having breakfast?" he asked when it became obvious that Mr. Crowder was not looking over the menu himself. Marc was an American who headed a company that competed with Mr. Crowder's firm, but they had always been friends. After he had surveyed the menu and made his order, he came to the point.

"I heard something about it. So they're closing down the Hong Kong operations entirely? Not bad news for us, but what's going to happen to you? Are they going to transfer you to Tokyo?"

"Apparently not. Seems like there is a worldwide cutback. We're being downsized. All of the local staff are being let go, and most of the expat staff too. I'm not sure if I can even find a place with the company back in the head office. They've been kind of vague on that." He paused a moment to take a sip from his coffee, then he continued.

"Marsha and I would prefer to stay in Hong Kong, at least a while longer. We've got the children in the International School, and it took them a while to get adjusted. Now they love it here." He paused, and said, "Marsha wouldn't mind moving back, though I think she would miss having Theresa . . ."

"Theresa?"

"Our domestic helper."

"Oh."

Gus hovered over them. "More coffee, sir?" Mr. Crowder shook his head, no. Marc motioned toward his cup, and Gus poured out more coffee. They sat in silence for a while.

"I'm not sure we can do much to help you," said Marc, answering the unasked question.

"We're getting all kinds of pressure from New York to keep costs down. The other day a directive came down that all new hires would be on local terms – no more housing subsidies, no more school fees, no more . . ." he swept his hand around in an expansive gesture, indicating the plush surroundings. "If I hired you as a manager, I might be able to give you sixty thousand."

Mr. Crowder smiled. Sixty thousand Hong Kong dollars a month would not cover even the monthly rent on No.10A Red Hill Drive, not to mention the children's school fees, club dues, living expenses – Theresa. Mr. Crowder had not really expected much, but he thought he should make the effort. There seemed no other solution but to go home, and do what he could there at his old firm. He told Mrs. Crowder this when he returned home from work that evening.

Theresa stepped out of the bus. It was Sunday, and the streets were crowded with people. Hundreds of Indonesian women walked toward Victoria Park, chatting among themselves. Theresa ignored them and walked purposefully down Paterson Street until she came to the right address. The sign above the narrow doorway said Garden Park Mansions, but it hardly looked like a mansion. She buzzed the door and walked in past the Chinese security guard – nodding over a wooden desk – and found the elevator. The elevator took her to the seventh floor, up past cheap hair salons and hotels with four or five rooms. She walked down a dingy, yellow-tiled corridor until she found the right door. There was no name over the buzzer, just an address. She pushed the buzzer, heard the metal door click open, and walked inside.

It was a kind of combination office and sorority house. She walked past the kitchen, where two Indonesian women were preparing a lunch on the wok. The aroma from the spicy food nearly overwhelmed her. She had almost forgotten what Indonesian food smelled like after several years cooking American food. On one side was a long leather sofa. Three women were lounging on it, watching the television set across the way. Above it hung a large map of Indonesia. On the other wide of the room were four desks with desktop computers on them. Theresa went to one of them and spoke to the woman behind it. She was Chinese but spoke Indonesian. "I need to see Mr. Chan," Theresa said. Looking up from the computer, the woman motioned her to take a seat. She joined the women sitting on the sofa and turned her attention to the television set, which was broadcasting an Indonesian program.

Theresa didn't especially like coming to her agency. She avoided it, except once every two years when she had to take care of the paperwork to renew her visa. For many other Indonesian women, however, it was a kind of home away from home. One of the bedrooms to the rear had been converted into a dormitory with half a dozen bunk beds for women who had been terminated or were waiting for new visas. Several women were lying on the bed, gossiping or reading Indonesian magazines. Theresa recoiled at the idea of joining them, but she knew her own situation was not that different. The day before, Mrs. Crowder had given her a termination letter. She had only two weeks to find another employer or go back home. She had already reserved a ticket through Dina, but still harbored some hopes. Mrs. Crowder had told her she would try to help her find a new employer from among her friends. She even posted a notice on the bulletin board at the American Club.

Theresa waited for two hours before she was told that Mr. Chan could see her. She walked down the corridor to his office. He was an Indonesian-Chinese, somewhat heavy set, wearing a batik shirt and seated behind a plain steel desk, cluttered with papers and piles of employment contracts.

"I don't think I can help you," Mr. Chan said, without any preliminary chat. He shuffled through some index cards on his desk. "I've got a dozen people in this office who have been terminated recently." As he said this he made a wide sweeping gesture with his right arm. Theresa's anger welled up. Anger at having to wait in this dingy office, anger at having to move her children out of the convent school, anger at the Crowders for moving back to America and leaving her without a job.

"You're my agent. You're supposed to help me. I paid you a lot of money."

Mr. Chan held up his hand. "Wait. You don't understand. A lot of people are losing jobs in Hong Kong now. Too many families are going back to where they came from. Just like yours. Maybe I can help you later."

"And you get another big fee? No thanks." Theresa heaved herself from the chair and stomped out of the room. She wished she could talk things over with Dina, but it was Sunday, and Dina was busy.

Moving day came to No. 10A Red Hill Drive. Cardboard boxes, rolls of tape, and packing paper were stashed everywhere. Mrs. Crowder darted around nervously, supervising the packers. Mr. Crowder was at the office that day winding up his affairs.

"Please be careful, that's an antique . . . Theresa!" she called. Theresa emerged from the kitchen where she had been supervising the packing of the dishes and the silverware. It must have been the twentieth time that morning that she had heard her name called in a loud plaintive voice. She came out of the living room and deftly took the situation in hand. "Theresa, I don't know what I'm going to do without you," Mrs. Crowder said again for about the twentieth time.

Theresa's own things were already packed. It had not taken her very long. Everything she owned, or wanted to take home, fit in her one suitcase and an oversized plastic bag. Some of the things were presents she had bought for her children. She had given the small television set to the maid who worked next door. Mr. Crowder had told her that he would drive her to the airport in his car, so she would not have to manhandle her suitcase and plastic bag onto the bus. She surveyed the tiny room that had been her home for the last five years. The bed was still there. Nobody had wanted to buy it; a charity would pick it up the next day.

In the morning Theresa took the bus to Victoria Park. She found Dina sitting at her usual spot.

"I have your ticket, *mbak*," she said as Theresa sat down on the bench beside her. Dina took the ticket out of her handbag and handed it over. Theresa looked at the details and held it in her lap.

"What are you doing with your children? Have you decided yet?" Dina asked, at length.

"They're going to stay with my cousin's family in Jakarta until the end of the term. Then we'll move them back to our town. I wish they could have finished . . . Sukemi was only one year away from graduation."

"Maybe you can get back here soon."

"Mr. Chan told me to check with his brother in Jakarta, but . . . " She didn't continue. Dina didn't have much else to say either. At length, Theresa thrust the ticket into her handbag and stood up. She gave Dina a little nod and walked out of the park.

14.

SPOILED GOODS

Although it was Sunday the Malang Restaurant was only half full. At one of the back tables Indonesian women were holding a party – talking and laughing among themselves. Entering, Rohaida thought she saw one of her friends and was about to turn away and leave when she realized that it was somebody else, a stranger. Even so, she moved to the far end of the restaurant, to an inconspicuous corner with a small table and seating for two. She didn't want to draw attention to herself, even though she hoped that Johnny wouldn't have trouble finding her. "I'll meet you at three at our old place," he had said when he called her on her mobile phone the night before. Rohaida had been surprised to hear his voice after all these months. For a few moments, she said nothing. "Are you there?" he had asked. "Yes," she had whispered. "I'm still here."

Rohaida settled into the seat, set her handbag down and looked at her watch. It was 2:30 p.m. She had made a point of coming early since she felt she needed time to compose herself before Johnny showed up. If he showed up. A waitress she had never seen before placed a menu in front of her and filled her water glass. Rohaida told her that she was waiting for somebody and would order later. She fingered the menu looking at the familiar dishes. Johnny had usually let her do the ordering, since he didn't know much about Indonesian food. She had known most of the waitresses before, but that was a long time ago, and she didn't go to the Malang Restaurant by herself any more. Now she usually bought a box of rice in Victoria Park and ate it alone on Sunday, or occasionally with some of her friends.

She had met Johnny at the Malang restaurant about a year after settling into Hong Kong. She was sitting with some of her friends when he and his friends entered the restaurant, laughing and joking. They sat down next to Rohaida's group, and Johnny asked her, "maybe you can help us order." She had advised him to order fried rice and chicken satay. They continued talking, and Johnny had passed his phone number to her. They met on Sunday, her day off, usually eating at the Malang or one of the other Indonesian restaurants in Causeway Bay. A few times Johnny took Rohaida to eat dim sum, and once he brought her home to the apartment he still shared with his parents. They had been polite and distant but also pleased that she could speak some Cantonese.

Rohaida remembered how her own family had reacted when she brought Johnny back to her home village. There were not very many Chinese, not even Indonesian-Chinese, living near her place. Her parents had been dismayed when she had written to them that she was bringing home a Chinese man that she had met in Hong Kong. They were even more dismayed when she said they planned to marry. Nevertheless, Johnny had tried hard to impress her family. He brought presents for her mother and two sisters. He had ridden a motorcycle with her brother. He was quiet and respectful to her parents. Before long the family had become reconciled to the idea of having a Chinese man in the family. The fact that he was a bank manager and that he had agreed to take part in a Muslim ceremony also helped to persuade them. Pretty soon they were introducing Johnny to their relatives, friends and neighbors as Rohaida's future husband.

So when Johnny abruptly called off the engagement a couple months after they returned to Hong Kong, she was humiliated. How could she explain what had happened, how it was *his* family that had objected to him marrying a foreign maid? For months she parried her mother's letters inquiring when she and Johnny would be coming back to Indonesia for the wedding. Rohaida put them off with various excuses. She was deeply reluctant to tell them the truth. In the eyes of her relatives and neighbors she would be spoiled goods.

Rohaida glanced at her watch again. It was past three. No sign yet of Johnny. Was he going to stand her up again? When they were going together he was usually so punctual. She picked up the menu once again and began reading the entries. Suddenly, she sensed somebody standing next to her and looked up.

"Hello, Rohaida," said Johnny.

She dropped her menu, knocking over her glass of water.

"Oh, no," she exclaimed as some of the water splashed onto Johnny's trousers. He laughed and dabbed the pants with a napkin. The waitress appeared quickly, picked up the glass and filled it with water. Johnny sat down across the table from her.

"It's nice to see you again," Rohaida said. "How are your parents?"

"They're okay," he said not eager to open that subject. Instead, Johnny picked up the menu and started reading it. Rohaida looked at Johnny appraisingly. He had grown a small thin mustache, which made him seem a little older. He had always looked to her like a boy, even though he was 34. She wondered what would have happened if she had stayed in her village. Her thoughts were interrupted as the waitress came over to the table, her pad in hand.

"Do you still like Ice?" she enquired of Johnny. An Indonesian concoction like a milk shake, it was one of Johnny's favorites. She spoke in Indonesian to the waitress, who jotted down her order and retreated to the kitchen. A minute later she returned and set the large frosty glass in front of Johnny and soon after the food arrived – *nasi goreng*, with a side order of chicken satay. Johnny tucked into it heartily. It was his favorite.

"I forgot how good it is here," Johnny said.

Johnny slid the last piece of meat sideways off of the skewer and put the stick down on the plate. "I was a little surprised that you still had the same phone number," he said.

"I'm surprised that you still remembered it. Didn't you throw it away when you threw me away?"

"Rohaida." Johnny looked around the restaurant noting that it had become even more crowded with Indonesian women as the hour had passed.

"Maybe we should go someplace else." he ventured.

Rohaida remembered when "someplace else" had meant going to a nearby guest hotel. They had usually met in the afternoon. Then, after lunch, they would go to the guest hotel and later – if there was still time before Rohaida's curfew – to one of the discos in Wanchai. Except for one time, Johnny never took her back to his place, and of course, Rohaida couldn't take him back to her employer's home.

"No, not there." Johnny was reading her mind. "Let's go out somewhere else, where we can talk."

Johnny paid the bill, and the two of them rose from their seats and walked out. One of the Indonesian women that Rohaida knew followed them with her eyes and gave Rohaida a brief smile. They walked silently toward Victoria Park – still teeming with people in the late afternoon. They crossed over the highway to the section that fronted the yacht basin, passing by Dina, who was busy cutting the hair of a woman sitting on the park bench that served as her makeshift outdoor salon. They walked further down the concrete quay until they found an empty bench and sat down. Rohaida stared at the pleasure boats bobbing in the water. A small garbage junk chugged among them, with an old Chinese woman in the bow, picking up the trash and debris floating on the surface.

"I thought about calling you before," Johnny broke the silence.

"Oh, why didn't you?"

"I didn't know how you would react, you know, after I broke off the engagement. What did you tell your parents?"

"I didn't tell them anything. I just made up a lot of excuses: you were too busy traveling in China, something like that."

She paused a few moments then continued.

"You don't know how hard it was for me to convince them to accept you. And when they finally did, you turned me down. How could I face them?"

"I'm sorry," Johnny said. "So you didn't tell them anything?"

"No. I've been scared to tell them. They would think I'm spoiled goods."

"Spoiled goods?" Johnny asked.

"I mean I lost too much face. Sometimes I wish I had never come out here. My sisters are already married and my oldest sister has two children."

"But you still have to send them money every month to help support them, don't you?"

"They were excited that I might marry a rich Hong Kong man."

"I'm not rich." – Johnny worked as the assistant manager of a small neighborhood branch of a large Hong Kong bank.

"They don't know that. I told them you were a big bank manager." They both laughed, then fell silent. They looked out over the harbor. A cruise liner was crossing in front of them, making its way down the channel. They could hear seagulls honking. It was getting late. Long shadows were being cast along the concrete embankment.

Johnny glanced at his watch. He had promised that he would join his parents at a restaurant for dinner that night at six. For a moment, he thought about asking Rohaida to join him, but decided against it. Not this time.

Johnny rose from the bench. "Rohaida . . ."

"Yes, I understand. You have to meet your parents," she guessed. Will . . . will I see you again?"

"Of course. Call me. You still have my number at the bank."

Yes, she still carried his business card around in her purse. For some reason she had never thrown it away. He got up to walk out of the park, but Rohaida told him she wanted to stay behind and talk with Dina.

"Dina?"

"The Indonesian woman who cuts hair in the park. She's over there," she said gesturing with her head. Johnny nodded that he understood, and with a brief wave he walked away.

Rohaida lingered a few moments longer on the bench, then she got up and walked over to Dina's place.

Dina was sweeping the concrete around her bench with a wicker broom, collecting the black strands of fallen hair into one large clump. Then she gathered it up in her hands and took it over to the waste bin.

"Hi, Dina," Rohaida said as she sat down on the bench. Dina sat down beside her, welcoming a chance to rest a few moments. She had been on her feet all day.

"Is that the guy?" Dina asked. She had, of course, noticed Johnny when the two of them walked into the beach.

"No" Rohaida replied guessing what Dina was talking about. "He's an old friend." She didn't tell Dina that she had been engaged to him and that he had thrown her over. Not that Dina would have been shocked.

"Do you have the tablets?" Rohaida abruptly changed the subject.

"No, not with me now. You can come back to my place with me if you want, and I'll give them to you. Or, I'll meet you later in the park."

"Maybe I'll walk back with you, if it is alright."

Dina stared out over the bobbing pleasure boats of the yacht basin for a few more moments, then she stuffed her tools, her scissors, and silk covering, into a plastic bag. She gathered them up with her handbag and stood up.

"Let's go."

Rohaida rose slowly and followed Dina. They walked silently together, climbing the stairs of the overpass over the freeway and down into Victoria Park – still crowded with Indonesian women. They waited for the light to change before crossing into Causeway Bay. They walked the two blocks to Dina's apartment.

Inside, Dina tossed her bags in a corner and told Rohaida to sit down on the sofa bed. Then she rummaged through her closet drawer and pulled out the medicine in a plastic wrapper. "Here you are," she said, and passed it to Rohaida.

Rohaida asked, "where do you get these?"

"I buy them from a guy who gets them in China." Then Dina asked, "are you sure about . . . ?"

"Yes, about two weeks" Rohaida replied. "I went over to family planning last Wednesday."

"What about the guy?"

"He doesn't know about it." And Rohaida wasn't planning to tell him either. An image of Sudhir came to her mind – a charming, tall, Pakistani man, who sold tape cassettes in Victoria Park. Rohaida suspected he had a couple other girlfriends whom he saw during the week when she was working. No, she wasn't planning to tell him anything.

Dina explained how to use the tablets. Rohaida listened and then extracted eight hundred dollars from her purse and handed the notes over. They sat together for a few more moments, silently. Then Dina got up and began shuffling through her stacks of magazines, getting ready to return to Victoria Park. Rohaida got up, said goodbye and left Dina's apartment.

She walked through the late afternoon crowds to her regular bus stop. The line was steadily growing longer, with other Indonesian maids returning to their homes before their curfews. The bus pulled up and the doors swung open. Rohaida climbed onto the second deck and found a seat up front. The bus pulled away and headed for the tunnel under Victoria Harbor that led to Kowloon. She opened her purse and found Johnny's card nestled next to the package of abortion tablets. She took the card out and turned it over looking at the English and Chinese words. Then she put it back in her handbag. She knew then that she probably wasn't going to call him again. After all, she was spoiled goods.

15.

WATI AND MURTINI

It wasn't the first time that Wati and Murtini quarreled. They spent all day together, so it would have been unusual if they did not have their little spats from time-to-time. Wati, in particular, had a sharp tongue and often made rude comments about the people who passed through Victoria Park, some of whom were Murtini's friends. Sometimes Murtini joined in the banter – there wasn't much else to do to pass the long hours spent sitting on the park bench, waiting for customers.

Moreover, the two women were competitors. Wati sold phonecards and exchanged money. Murtini did that, but also made and sold lunch boxes filled with fried rice, which she prepared every morning in the tiny apartment she shared with two other women. Wati usually arrived first, sometimes as early as 8.30 a.m., staking out her place on the bench near the park's southeastern entrance. Most people passing by naturally assumed she was just another middle-aged woman whiling away the day in the park. She carried her phonecards and wads of rupiah notes in a large handbag. Murtini usually arrived an hour later, toting a plastic bag filled with white Styrofoam lunch boxes. She sat down on the bench and plopped her plastic bag down beside her.

By the time Murtini arrived, Victoria Park was coming alive. Streams of Chinese exited the buses and walked across the park to their places of work. The two women ignored the Chinese, looking for the odd Indonesian, a maid with a day off, or the wife of a Hong Kong resident. They whispered discretely: "*kartu telpon, rupiah.*" Sometimes the women stopped and spent a few minutes chatting with Wati, since she was the more voluble of the two. Murtini was quieter, and perhaps for this reason sold fewer phonecards than her friend. She made up for it by selling the lunch boxes. She was especially busy on Sunday, when Victoria Park overflowed with domestic helpers. She often had to make several trips back to her apartment to get more boxes, or pay one of her friends to get them for her, so that she would not have to leave and lose sales to Wati.

They had known each other since they were children, coming from the same small town in central Java. Indeed, it was Wati who had persuaded Murtini to come out to Hong Kong. Wati had left a husband back in Indonesia and two children, who were almost grown – The remittances that she earned from selling phonecards and changing money helped pay for their schooling. But she also had a boyfriend in Hong Kong – a Pakistani man. They quarreled frequently, and she bored Murtini with tales of her boyfriend's unfaithfulness, and when she dozed off, Wati continued talking with the other women in the tiny apartment.

During the day they kept a wary eye out for security, since neither of them had a hawker's license. It would have been impossible for either of them to obtain one legally, since, technically, they were in Hong Kong as domestic helpers and were not permitted to work outside of the home of their employer. They both paid a substantial sum to a Chinese man who posed as their employer. If any policeman asked why they were not at work, they would tell him that it was their day off, or that their employer had left Hong Kong for an extended vacation and they had little to do. That happened from time to time, but so far, their story had always been accepted. Most of the security people who patrolled the park knew Wati and Murtini and usually left them alone. But occasionally they ran into somebody new or overzealous.

Wati had been arrested once before. It happened on a busy Sunday morning as she was standing outside the entrance to the subway exit, selling phonecards to the Indonesian women streaming out of the portal. She was so engrossed in what she was doing that she did not see the police officer watching her, until she suddenly felt his tap on her shoulder. He gave her a ticket and told her to report to the court the following Thursday. For the next few days Wati lived in terror that she would end up in jail, or worse, even be deported. She stayed in her room all day, fearful of going out to the park, and those who saw her said she was unusually quiet. But on the day she appeared in court, she was merely fined 500 Hong Kong dollars and given a lecture by the judge about taking away somebody else's employment during difficult economic times. The next day she was back in Victoria Park sitting in her familiar spot, joking and gossiping with her friends.

The quarrel began late one morning in the middle of the week. Wati and Murtini were sitting in their usual place on the bench in front of the big tree. Business had been good all morning for Murtini. She had sold more than twenty phonecards, and people were beginning to buy some of her lunch boxes as the clock was approaching noon. Business had not gone so well for Wati, who spent most of the time talking with Retno. After a while, Retno left the bench, while two more Indonesian women came up to Murtini. One purchased a phonecard, the other changed 500 Hong Kong dollars into rupiah. Wati sat in silence.

A few minutes later Wati's mobile phone rang. She listened intently without saying anything, then snapped the phone shut and turned to Murtini.

"That was Retno. She says the police are in the park, looking for drug dealers and anyone else who shouldn't be here. We'd better get out."

With that Wati heaved her bulk from the bench, grabbed her handbag and waddled out of the park into Causeway Bay.

Murtini sat quietly for a while, uncertain about what to do. She peered deeply into the park trying to see if there were any police or security people there. She wished she could talk to Dina, but she had returned to her place to cut hair. Murtini reflected that Wati had been arrested once before and perhaps was being overcautious. She looked at the plastic satchel stuffed with unsold lunch boxes. They would be pretty obvious. Finally, she made up her mind: She grabbed her lunch boxes and handbag, walked quickly from the park to the subway, and back to her small apartment.

She spent the rest of the day in her tiny room, lying on her bed watching Chinese soap operas on television. The next morning she went to the park as usual. Wati was late, for some reason, and Murtini fell into conversation with Dina, who was sitting at her regular spot. Murtini was not usually very friendly with Dina, but she was curious about what had happened the day before.

"I heard there was some trouble in the park yesterday," Murtini ventured.

"Oh? What kind of trouble? I didn't hear anything," Dina replied.

Murtini was a little surprised. "Wati said the police made a big raid, looking for drug dealers and hawkers."

"Oh, that was nothing. I think security may have warned a couple of old men who were gambling."

"But Wati and I went back to our places, just in case. Didn't you?"

"No. Why should I? And I remember Wati was here all afternoon. She seemed to be doing a lot of business. We both were. I wondered why you had left."

Murtini stewed about this information all day. She didn't say a word to Wati, who also ignored her for the rest of the day. But as soon as she got home that evening, she called Dina and vented her frustrations.

"She made up that story about the police just so I would leave the park and she wouldn't have any competition from me," she began . . .

"Well, there were police . . . "

"You told me already that it was nothing but a few old men gambling . . . I wish I could punch her face."

"You know that if you do anything to hurt Wati, Najib will hurt you back, maybe hard." Najib was Wati's boyfriend, a burly Pakistani man who sometimes sold music cassettes in the park on his day off.

"She's always talking about me to the other women. Anything I say to her she just repeats to everyone."

"I know," said Dina, who had also felt Wati's tongue.

"Maybe I will just tell Immigration about her. She can go back to Indonesia, and I won't have to listen to her any more."

"You know you can't do that," replied Dina. "If you turn her in to Immigration, she'll just do the same thing to you."

"I don't care," Murtini said and snapped her phone shut.

Of course, she did care. She needed the money she made in Hong Kong. Her family back home depended on it. And she knew she couldn't turn in Wati. She went fitfully to sleep dreaming of other ways of revenge.

But in the end she did nothing. There was really nothing she could do. Dina was right, of course. It would have been worse than useless to turn Wati in to the authorities. All through the week the two women studiously ignored each other. Wati sat at the far end of the bench, talking with her friends and occasionally tossing a glance that Murtini thought looked like a smirk.

One day however, Wati failed to appear as usual. She was gone for the entire day. This wasn't so unusual, Wati occasionally took the day off, lying around in her cramped apartment or sometimes going to the beach during the summer.

But when she failed to appear over the next three days, Murtini got curious. She spotted Retno crossing into the park from under the overpass and waved her over.

"What's happened to your friend – she won the Mark Six?" Murtini affected nonchalance.

"Didn't you hear? Wati was arrested three days ago. Immigration came to her apartment and took her and two other overstays who were with her. She's got to go to court tomorrow."

"Didn't she tell them to call Steven?" Steven was the Chinese man who posed as Wati's employer."

"Yes, but he refused to back up Wati's story – he's got tax problems and didn't want to get into any more trouble. She said some bad things about you too, she thinks you're the one who set her up, to make up for the time she cheated you in the park." It was the first time anyone had admitted the ruse.

"But . . . she can't believe that," Murtini stammered . . . Retno just shrugged.

The next day Murtini took the subway to the Eastern Magistrate's Court. The foyer was crowded with people, half of them, it seemed, Filipinas, with a sprinkling of Indonesian women. She found the right courtroom and took her place on one of the rows of wooden benches toward the back. She could see Wati sitting alone, several rows in front of her. Her boyfriend had not accompanied her to the trial. Everyone rose as the judge, an Englishman, entered and took his place at the bench.

"Sri Simawati," the bailiff finally intoned, and, after a moment's hesitation, she walked slowly in front of the bench. The Indonesian translator moved beside her. The judge read out the indictment and asked Wati if she were guilty or not guilty. She waited for the translation and then whispered "guilty" in English.

"Convicted," the judge said. "Two months in jail, suspended. And deportation." It had all taken less than three minutes.

As Wati moved away from the center, she caught sight of Murtini sitting in the back row. She stared at her for a full second, then mouthed, "I'll get you back." Murtini shook her head and said, "it wasn't me," but by then Wati had left the courtroom.

Murtini lived in constant fear that Wati had turned her in to the authorities. She stayed away from her boarding house, sleeping on the floor of one of her friends' room. She was afraid that the authorities would raid that place too, so she sometimes spent the night sleeping on the ground in Victoria Park. She went back to her room only to change her clothes and sometimes to take a quick shower. She gave up cooking her lunch boxes, since it required that she spend too much time in her place. She lived just on the sales of phonecards, and money changing.

Murtini was so absorbed in trying to avoid Immigration that she became careless at her job. And one day as she was fumbling through her purse to pull out a phonecard to sell to a customer, she felt the tap on her shoulder. She turned in horror to see a stern-looking security guard hovering over her.

Five days later, Murtini found herself in the same courtroom where only a few weeks previously Wati had been sentenced and deported. The charge – illegal hawking – normally should have carried no more than a 1,000 Hong Kong dollar fine. But the judge noted that Murtini had been arrested on a Wednesday, when she was supposed to be in a home ironing clothes or looking after the baby. Poor Murtini was too downcast, too tired, too scared, to come up with any plausible excuse why she was sitting in a public park in the middle of a working day. Why her purse was stuffed with phonecards and millions in rupiah notes. She scarcely nodded as the court translator repeated the judge's sentence – two months in jail, suspended, and deportation back to Indonesia.

A few weeks later, Wati and Murtini were again sitting side-by-side, this time in a market place in their home village in Java. Wati had a crude cooler from which she sold bottles of soft drinks and cigarettes. Murtini prepared and sold her lunch boxes. Nobody cared for phonecards or rupiah notes. They sat on the ground on a plastic sheet, and a kind of tent covered them from the heat and the sun. Every now and then Wati lifted a fat hand to swat a fly, or make a rude comment about somebody passing by. Murtini just sat there in silence.

16.

TAKE A NUMBER

For the tenth time that morning, Wiji looked at the piece of paper she was holding in her lap, then compared it with the number on the screen. The number had not changed since the last time she looked – 65. The number on the paper in her hand was 75. Wiji had been sitting for nearly an hour in the visa section of the British Consulate. She had arrived promptly at 9 a.m., and now it was a little past 10 a.m., and it looked like she might have to sit there for another hour before her number was called. She had told her employer that she had to go to Immigration, but had not specified which Immigration. The woman had looked at her strangely – her contract as a domestic helper was not near expiry – but had said nothing.

She picked up a magazine lying beside her on an empty chair, and thumbed through the pages, looking at pictures of large country houses in lush green settings. William lived somewhere in the country, he'd said, though she doubted that his home looked like the ones in the magazine. She tried to imagine what the small town he lived in looked like. "It's about twenty miles north of London," he had told her. But the only images that came to her mind were of her own small town in Java, and she was sure that his place would be nothing like that.

She continued to finger the magazine's glossy pages, pictures of Buckingham Palace with the red-coated guards and their big bushy hats, pictures of empty islands in northern Scotland. Once again, she wondered what life would be like living in such a place, halfway around the world. Of course, William had been enthusiastic about it the last time he was in Hong Kong.

"You'll love it in England," he had exclaimed, lying in bed, with his body propped up by an arm.

"Are there any other Indonesian women in this place you live?"

"Oh, I'm sure there are," he said vaguely. "We have a lot of nannies from Asia."

Wiji wasn't convinced. She had never heard of any of her friends moving to England to work or live. She hardly knew of anyone who had ever been to Europe. One of her friends had tried to get a visa to visit Paris to see her French boyfriend, but she had been denied entry because she was young and single. Wiji looked at the screen again. The number had advanced to 67. She sighed and put the magazine down on the seat next to her.

Compared with other domestic helpers in Hong Kong, Wiji was a pretty experienced traveler. She had been to the Gold Coast of Australia with Trevor, and to Bali two times, once with Stephen, and again with William. Only a few months ago, she had spent a long weekend in Phuket with William. But these destinations were all close to Hong Kong and the visits were short. The idea of moving permanently to England to live near William was something else.

"But I won't be able to stay with you, when I'm there," Wiji had wailed, when William first broached the idea. They were lying in bed at the hotel where William usually stayed.

"No, but you will be close to me. I've already checked with the agency, and they say there are many people looking for nannies in my town. They said they could find a place for you easily. You would get a permit to stay for six months, at first. After that, you could get a longer one. We could be together."

"But I would have to give up my job in Hong Kong," Wiji protested.

"So?" William replied. "Anyway, you would be doing what you are doing now, taking care of children – except that you wouldn't have to cook or clean the house, or . . ."

Wiji had said nothing more for while. She liked her life in Hong Kong. Her employers – a Danish couple – were very liberal with her, allowing her to go out at night after she had prepared the dinner, unlike many of her friends who had a curfew, even on their day off. That was why she could stay with William when he was in town. It was why she could go to the discos when he was out of town. And, of course, she had many friends she could gossip with in Victoria Park on Sunday. Why should she give up that to move to England?

Wiji glanced back at the screen again. The number had advanced to 69, but she couldn't remember hearing any names called. It was spookily quiet in the large room, except for the low murmuring of voices from the people waiting, or sitting at the counters talking with immigration officers. She looked around the room. Most of the people were Chinese, with a sprinkling of Westerners and South Asians. The women dressed in bright red and green saris. As far as she could see, there were no other Indonesians. She felt very much alone. She wished that William was there with her, but he was back in the UK.

"You'll do fine. Just relax and be yourself," he had said encouragingly when she had talked with him long-distance that morning.

She had asked Dina to come and sit with her, but she was reluctant to take that much time away from her business, even on a workday, when things were usually slow in Victoria Park. "I can't leave this spot for a whole morning, *mbak*," she had said when Wiji had come by the park on her day off. "You should be okay. You have a letter from the agency, right?"

Wiji had the letter in her purse. She opened the bag and withdrew the envelope with the single sheet of paper inside. At the top was the letterhead for the recruitment agency addressed "To Whom it May Concern." It contained only a few lines requesting favorable attention to Ms Wiji Astuti's request for a six-month work permit to work as a nanny in the household of . . . It listed the name and address.

"It looks pretty good to me," said Dina, after she had absorbed the words. She carefully folded the letter and handed it back to Wiji, who placed it back in the envelope and stuffed it back in her bag. Then she stared silently across the park, before speaking again.

"Do you think that Immigration here will double check with the agency in England?" she said finally.

"I don't know. William said not to worry about it. Just show the letter to Immigration and everything will be okay."

"Well, maybe he's right. Anyway, the worst that can happen is that you'll be turned down," Dina said finally.

"Maybe that would be best," said Wiji.

The screen had just flipped to 72. It wouldn't be long before her number was called. Wiji thought about simply getting up and walking out of the room, back to her employer's apartment, back to her comfortable little room, back to her familiar household chores. But then, of course, she wondered what she would tell William when he called her that night. She remembered what Dina had said, "the worst that can happen is that you'll be turned down."

Wiji settled back in her chair. It was almost 11 a.m. With any luck she could be finished by noon. Maybe she could spend an hour window shopping in the nearby mall, before she was missed back at home. The number changed to 73 with a soft click.

The night before, Wiji had had trouble sleeping. She lay in her bed in the small maid's room, staring at the ceiling. After a few hours she finally fell asleep. In her dream she was sitting at the immigration counter, except that the person behind the counter wasn't an immigration officer. It was her mother – a diminutive woman with a worn, leathery face – wearing a dark brown hair scarf. "Wiji, why do you want to go to England? It's so far away," her mother was saying, and she seemed to reach through the glass partition to clutch her hands. The image faded away to be replaced by Jurur, the Indonesian man her mother wanted her to marry. "Why are you going away so far, Wiji? Come home. I'll take care of you." Then again, that image faded, and a new apparition appeared behind the counter. It was William, smiling at her, beckoning her to come. "Don't worry. Everything will be okay." And he seemed to pull her through the partition.

"Wiji Astuti." The sound of her name coming over the intercom jolted her from her reverie. "Wiji Astuti, counter seven," the voice repeated. Slowly, Wiji rose to her feet, grabbed her handbag and headed for counter seven, at the far end of the room. She sat down on the stool, her handbag in her lap.

She half expected to see her mother behind the partition. Instead, she faced a kindly-looking, middle-aged Western woman, who smiled at her when she sat down, and murmured "good morning." Wiji began to relax a little. Perhaps this wasn't going to be such an ordeal.

Ten minutes later she rose from the stool and walked away. The woman behind the partition had examined her letter from the nanny agency, stuck it in her folder and asked some questions about how long she had been working in Hong Kong, how many children she handled, and whether she had any relatives living in Britain. She cheerfully ended the interview by telling Wiji that she would be notified about her work permit in two weeks. Wiji walked out of the Consulate feeling that a load had been lifted. Her future was out of her hands. She would either get the permit or be denied. She would either go to England or stay in Hong Kong. It was in the hands of God.

One month later, Wiji stood in line, gradually nudging her baggage cart towards the airline check-in counter. On it were two suitcases and a large striped plastic bag. They held all of the things she had acquired in Hong Kong, save the stereo set William had bought her, which she had sold to Leila. Her employer had been understanding when she had given notice. They had already hired a replacement who would be flying in from Indonesia in a few weeks.

Dina was standing next to her. She was the only one of her friends to come see her off. It was a week day, and everyone else was working. But she did have a kind of farewell dinner the previous Sunday at an Indonesian restaurant in Causeway Bay. Her friends had teased her about having to give up her boyfriends in Hong Kong.

"Have you got your ticket?" Dina asked, breaking the silence. Wiji looked into her purse once again. It was nestled against her passport and mobile phone.

"Jurur said his brother would meet me at the airport, when I get to Jakarta," Wiji said, suddenly changing the subject. "The wedding is next month."

"How did William take your decision to go home?"

Wiji grimaced and said, "I was afraid to tell him, so I finally wrote him a long email. He called me back four times that night."

The line had reached the counter, and Dina stopped talking while Wiji got her boarding pass and checked her baggage. Then they walked over to the boarding gate.

"I forgot to ask whether you ever got your permit to live in England?"

"Oh, yes, one year," Wiji said. Then she waved goodbye and disappeared through the gate.

17.

RETNO GETS RELIGION

A nudge on the shoulder jolted Retno from her fitful sleep. She opened her eyes and looked up at Corinne, the Filipina bartender. "You better get up now. We're closing," Corrine said, and then walked away. Retno looked around her. The musicians had already packed up their instruments and left the small stage in front of the dance floor. The women who cruised the bar waiting for customers had left. Most of the sofas around her were deserted. She opened the purse next to her and found two drinks tickets. She searched her memory but couldn't remember the face of the man who had bought her drinks, not that she could see him that clearly in the dark. But a ticket was a ticket, and Retno heaved her body from the sofa and walked over to the bar and placed them on the counter. Joe, the Chinese barman, wordlessly exchanged them for a hundred-dollar note. Retno placed it in her bag, waved goodbye to Corinne and walked up the stairs.

It was already daylight when she emerged from the dark dungeon of the disco. She held a hand in front of her eyes until they adjusted to the sunlight. As she walked up Luard Road, she could hear the metallic rattle and thump as the steel door gate was lowered behind her. On the corner of Luard and Lockhart Roads a forlorn looking hooker was still standing her post, slumping slightly from fatigue and hoping for one last late customer. But there were no men anywhere in sight at this hour.

Retno passed by the Chinese noodle shop, and, feeling hungry, went inside. She exchanged her hundred-dollar note for twenty dollars worth of noodles and a hot cup of Chinese tea. She felt sluggish and cramped from two hours spent sleeping on the sofa, but the hot tea revived her somewhat, as did the warm noodles. In one corner she saw three Filipina girls – off duty from a night in one of the girly bars – eating breakfast before returning to their lodgings. They had exchanged their rhinestones and platform boots for plain jeans and tennis shoes. Retno watched as they laughed and gossiped together. A few minutes later they got up and left the noodle shop.

Retno finished her noodles, drank the last of the tea, and walked out onto Lockhart Road. Having no permanent lodging of her own, her feet naturally pulled her in the direction of Victoria Park. Causeway Bay was already growing crowded with Indonesian women, streaming from the subways and buses. It was Sunday, their day off. Retno preferred to spend weekdays in Victoria Park, when there were fewer people, passing the day talking and gossiping with her friends. On Sunday there were so many faces and it was hard to find anybody she knew. She entered the park – already filling with people – walked past the model-boat pond, found her favorite grassy spot on the knoll, and lay down. She quickly fell asleep.

When Retno awoke, the sun was already high in the sky. Her body felt stiff and sore as she struggled to her feet, the result of a night spent slumped on a disco sofa, and later, on the hard ground of Victoria Park. She walked along the parkway back past the model-boat pond, now buzzing with toy speedboats. Not far from the pond she spotted a circle of eight or ten Indonesian women sitting together. All of them were wearing headscarves, and each held in her hand a book in Arabic. Retno lingered for a few moments, watching the young women in their Koran study. Retno was a Muslim, but she normally did not observe all the rituals of her faith. She had not even fasted during Ramadan a few months before. One of the women looked up at her and smiled, but Retno moved away toward the concrete soccer field.

She spotted Dina at her usual spot under the big tree, an array of magazines spread out in front of her. She thought about stopping to chat, but she knew that Dina was usually very busy on Sundays. Instead, she walked onto the soccer pitch, attracted by a large crowd of women watching something that was going on a stage at the far end of the pitch. She edged closer to see and hear what was happening. A Filipino man was exhorting the crowd through a microphone – his voice greatly amplified by the two black cubes of the public address system. Behind him were several other men with guitars hanging around their necks.

They looked sort of like the combo that played regularly at the Big Apple, but the message was very different. Retno listened for a while, curious as to what was going on.

"Eternity is a very long time, my friends," the speaker was shouting through the microphone. "The fires of hell are as old and everlasting as God himself. Oh my friends your minds are too small to grasp what it means to be in eternity."

"Amen" the women in the crowd shouted together, a few of them raised their arms and waved them back and forth. Retno was about to turn away from the crowd when she spotted Emy among them. She was surprised to see any Indonesian woman at a Christian revival, much less somebody that she knew. She walked over to where Emmy was standing and said, "What are you doing here?"

If Emy was surprised to see Retno, she didn't show it. She simply gave Retno a big smile, and, putting an arm out, drew her closer.

"I'm happy to see you here. Isn't this wonderful?" she gushed.

"I didn't actually come here to see this," Retno stammered. "And what are you doing here?"

But before Emy could reply the band swung into another gospel song. She turned her attention back to the stage and started singing and clapping her hands with the rest of the crowd.

Retno lingered for a few more moments at the edge of the crowd, thinking about what she had seen. Then she walked back to where Dina was sitting, and plumped herself down on the bench beside her.

"Where have you been, *mbak*? You look agitated." Dina turned to her in a friendly way.

"I just got back from that rally over there . . ." She pointed back to the soccer pitch. The gospel music from the band was still clearly audible.

"Are you getting religion now?" Dina asked.

"No!" Retno said emphatically." I was just curious about what was going on. But then I saw Emy there. She was singing and clapping her hands with the group. I thought she was a Muslim. What was she doing there?"

"You know Emy. She just wanted to sing and dance a little, I suppose. You know, ever since Miriam transferred to another ship and the dance society broke up."

Retno pondered this for a few moments then said, "You're a Christian, aren't you?" Dina nodded. She had been educated in Catholic convent school. Sometimes she went to Mass during the weekdays. On Sundays she was too busy. She did not pick up on the subject, and a few moments later Retno got up, waved a short goodbye and headed out of the park. It was getting late, and already some women were leaving, some to go home, others to the discos. Retno avoided the discos on Sundays since they were packed with Filipina and Indonesian women.

She walked down Lockhart Road, back toward Wanchai, retracing the steps she had followed in the morning. She found the entrance to Sussy's boarding house, pushed the door code and entered the corridor. Sussy let her stash her things, in her suitcase, in a corner of her lodging. She found her suitcase, placed her handbag down beside it and rummaged through it for some clean clothes.

A few days later, Retno was back in Victoria Park, sitting by herself on a bench close to the west entrance to the park. The early spring weather had turned cool again, and Sussy had let her sleep on the floor of her boarding house for the past two nights. She had spent her evenings in the Big Apple, but traffic was sparse. In the two evenings, she only picked up one drink, which added another fifty dollars to her dwindling money supply.

In the distance, she noticed a couple of *bule* approaching the park from Sugar Street. They were dressed identically in plain white shirts and black trousers, and carrying books in their hands. Both were about twenty years old and came from America, Retno thought. On the right breast each one sported a little black plastic name tag: Michael and Jeffrey – Mike and Jeff to the denizens of the park. At this distance, Retno could not make out the words, but she knew who they were anyway.

Retno remembered that Wati had told her they were Mormons, although she didn't know what that meant. For a while Retno confused them with Muslims, even though she didn't know why these two well-scrubbed young Americans would be Muslims. Wati claimed that they could have as many wives as they wanted, even more than the four allotted to Muslim men. "Maybe you can get one of them to marry you," she had told Retno. "Then you can go to America and join his other wives." Retno wasn't sure she believed Wati. She said a lot of stupid things. Wati had liked to tease the young men. "I'll meet you later in Wanchai," she joked. The young men took the bantering good-naturedly. Retno usually just kept quiet.

Retno noticed that the two young men were standing in front of her. The one named Mike, smiled at her and said, "Good Morning."

"Did you hear? Retno has become a Christian."

Sussy was sitting next to Dina in Victoria Park. It was late in the afternoon, a few weeks after Retno had met the Mormons.

"How do you know that?" asked Dina.

"I found this in her things," said Sussy, pulling out a pamphlet from her handbag. The cover headline read, "The Purpose of Life," and it had the profile of Jesus praying by himself. She handed the document over to Dina, who studied it intently, turning it over to the opposite page. At the bottom it read, "A publication of the Church of Jesus Christ of Latter Day Saints."

"What is that?" she asked.

"I don't know. Some kind of Christian organization."

"Maybe it was from those two *bule* who are always in the park."

"What *bule*?"

"Don't get excited." Dina replied. "They're not your type. Anyway this doesn't prove anything. Maybe she just took it and stuffed it in her purse."

"But I haven't seen her around for a couple weeks," Sussy replied. "I'm getting worried."

Later that evening Sussy dropped into the Big Apple. It was early in the week, and she fell into conversation with Corrine.

"Have you seen Retno?" she asked. "I haven't seen her for a couple weeks,"

"No, she hasn't been here. You mean she moved out of your place?"

"I don't know. Her things are still there."

Corrine merely shrugged and went off to serve a customer. "Maybe she's working some other disco," she called back. But Sussy had already been to several other discos that evening, and she had not seen Retno there either.

The next day Sussy rummaged through Retno's things. She found the pamphlet she had shown to Dina and looked at the bottom for the address. Then she took the bus to Caine Road. She stood a few moments looking at the imposing red-brick structure before entering. The sanctuary was empty as she walked down the center aisle, past the empty pews. To the left she spotted an open door and walked through it into the kitchen. There she saw a woman leaning over the sink and washing the dishes.

"Retno?" Sussy asked. Startled, Retno turned toward her, dropping the cup she was holding.

"Oh, Sussy," she said, relaxing a little. She picked up the cup and put it back in the tray. She dried her hands with a dishtowel. "What are you doing here?"

"We wondered where you were. Corrine said you haven't been to the disco in a couple weeks."

"I've stopped all of that," Retno replied.

'Oh, you got a job here . . . or, did you join the church?"

Retno did not reply directly. She led Sussy into a small room behind the kitchen where there was a small wardrobe and a cot. She sat down and Sussy sat down beside her.

"You know," she whispered confidentially, "I still won't eat any pork. I tell them I just don't like it."

"Retno came by my place yesterday and picked up the rest of her things to take back to the church." Sussy was sitting next to Dina in Victoria Park. "She said one of the Mormons is going to sign a contract so that she can work legally at the church."

"Do you think she really became a Mormon?" Dina asked.

"I don't know, but she whispered to me, 'I don't eat pork. I tell them it makes my stomach upset'."

Dina laughed. "I don't know if she's found God, but I think Retno has finally found a home."

18.

THE ARREST

Nick punched the numbers into his mobile phone, hoping, at least, to hear the familiar ring. Instead, he got the recording again: *The party you wish to talk to is unavailable at the moment. Please try again later.* He snapped the phone shut and looked at his watch. It was nearly seven. He had first got the recording when he called Dina at five, just after he left work. He had been only mildly irritated at the time. There were still a couple hours before they were to meet. He had called four times since then, every half hour, and had got the same recording. Now he was not only a little irritated; he was a little worried.

At first he thought that Dina was angry at him, but he couldn't think why. He had called her earlier in the day from work, and she had sounded cheerful. He searched his mind, imagining what he might have done to upset her. It was true that he had gone to that sports bar in Wanchai with some of his friends a few nights before, but he had told her about it, even if he didn't mention flirting with the Filipina waitress. As far as he could tell, no Indonesian women were there, so nobody would likely call her. He punched the number into the phone again, and again he got the message: "The party you wish to talk to is not available at the moment. Please try again later."

He closed the phone and put it in his pocket. He walked across Victoria Park. He exited the far side of the park, crossed the street and walked the two blocks to his apartment building. Inside he went to the refrigerator and pulled out a bottle of San Miguel. He placed his mobile phone on his bedroom dresser, vowing not to make another call, and sat down on the small sofa in the sitting room, turning on the television. Around eight he returned to the bedroom and picked up the phone again, but this time he put it down without making a call. A few minutes later it buzzed.

"Dina?"

"Nick?"

"Yes, darling. Where are you? I've been trying to call you all afternoon, but your phone is always turned off. Are you mad at me?"

Dina ignored the question, and after a short pause, her voice came back on the line. "I can't talk to you for very long . . . I'm at Immigration . . ."

"Immigration?" Nick replied. "What do you mean?"

"I was arrested. I can't talk to you now, they want me to hang up." Then the phone went dead.

"Dina!" Nick stammered, but he got only a dial tone in response. He looked at the caller display, but it offered no clues. He snapped the phone shut and sat back down on the sofa.

Where the hell was she? Dina had only talked vaguely about being at "Immigration."

Early next morning, Nick walked over to Victoria Park. The bench Dina usually sat on was occupied by a couple of Indonesian women he didn't recognize. He asked them if they knew Dina, but they shook their heads. He remembered that Dina's friend Nurma lived in a large apartment in Causeway Bay. She would know what to do, if only he could remember exactly where she lived.

Nurma looked surprised when she opened the door. Men rarely came by her place.

"Dina's been arrested," Nick blurted out even before he stepped inside.

"What? Who?" Nurma was still only half awake. She had been up late the night before.

"Dina. She says she's been arrested and held at Immigration," Nick repeated.

Nurma gestured him to come inside and directed him to sit on the black leather sofa, while she disappeared into her bedroom to put on a robe. A few of the other women in Nurma's place were puttering around in the kitchen. The boarding house was coming alive.

When she returned, Nick briefly told her about Dina's phone call the night before. Nurma listened quietly, then, without saying anything, picked up her mobile phone and made a couple of calls, speaking quietly in Indonesian. The she snapped the phone shut. "I talked with Elena, one of my friends. She said one of the security guards – he wasn't wearing any uniform – arrested Dina around 3 p.m. yesterday. She thinks he may have been watching her for an hour or so. Anyway they took her away in a van."

"Where is she now?" Nick asked.

"She doesn't know for sure but probably at Victoria Prison. That's where most of the immigration cases end up."

"Victoria Prison? Where's that?"

"It's in Central, on Hollywood Road."

"Oh." Nick had visited many of the bars along Hollywood Road and nearby streets but he did not remember the old prison. But Nurma had been there many times. She got up again and went back into her room to get dressed. "Wait here," she said, "We'll go down there together."

"I don't understand . . ." Nick said as they were riding toward Central in a taxi. He had insisted that they take a taxi rather than ride the bus. "Why arrest her now? She's been selling things at that spot for a long time. I thought they just tolerated her."

"I don't know for sure. Maybe it was somebody new." Or, maybe somebody turned her in, she thought to herself. Dina loaned money to a lot of the girls and she made enemies. Nurma had warned her about that before, but Dina insisted that she needed the money.

"What's likely to happen now?" Nick asked nervously.

"Maybe she will just get a fine," she replied. And maybe she will be sent home. It seemed strange to her that Immigration had taken the trouble to investigate her, like they were gathering evidence. Dina was well known, and it may be that they were gunning for her. At that moment the taxi pulled up to Central Police Headquarters and stopped. Nick handed the driver a hundred-dollar bill, and they got out of the car.

They walked up Old Bailey Street to the side entrance to the old gaol, Nurma pressed the buzzer and they entered into a kind of anteroom, were searched, and allowed to enter the visitor's room. Nurma talked quietly with the female corrections officer behind the counter, whispering Dina's name and when she was arrested. "There's nobody here by that name," the officer replied flipping through a folder.

"But we know that she was detained by Immigration," Nurma responded.

"Maybe she's at our Kowloon facility," the woman said and wrote down the address on a slip of paper.

"She's not here," Nurma told Nick.

The two of them left the prison and walked down the hill to the subway entrance, to take the train to Kowloon. Nick seldom visited Kowloon side, but Nurma knew where to find the Immigration office. They took another taxi after alighting at the subway station.

Again Nurma did the talking. A young Chinese corrections officer flipped through some papers. Then he spoke into a phone in Cantonese. Finally, he reported. "Yes, she is here."

"Is that all," Nick interrupted, and he began quizzing the officer in rapid English. Nurma waved him to be quiet and again turned to talk to the officer. "He doesn't speak English well," she explained. After a few more words, the officer handed her the phone. She gestured to Nick for a pencil and wrote something down on a scrap of paper. She returned the phone to the cradle and turned to Nick.

"They said she will appear tomorrow morning at the Central Kowloon Magistrate's Court."

Nick rose early the next morning and took the subway to Kowloon. A taxi deposited him in front of the imposing courthouse. He climbed the long concrete steps and entered the building. Inside, he remembered that he didn't know which courtroom Dina would be appearing in. Then he remembered that he didn't know her full name. She had always been just Dina to him. He went up to a woman in uniform and stammered out his query. She answered briskly, "The immigration cases are in Courtroom 3, 9 a.m." Nick looked at his watch. It was nearly nine. He found the courtroom and took a seat on one of the wooden benches near the front.

Presently, the English judge entered the courtroom and took his place on the bench. Everybody rose and bowed slightly towards him. Nick sat down, reflecting that he didn't know the docket number, and he had no idea when Dina's case would be heard. He could be there for a long time. Most of the cases seemed to involve immigration matters, mostly overstays, and the judge disposed of them as if on an assembly line. Few of the women spoke for themselves or had a lawyer. Lawyers. Nick wondered if he should have hired one, but then things had moved so fast, and he still didn't know exactly what Dina was charged with.

After sitting for nearly one hour, Nick became restless. He thought for a moment of leaving the courtroom and going out into the foyer to buy a soft drink from the machine. He reflected that he was supposed to go to work after lunch and had not remembered to call in sick. He was about to get up, when one of the side doors opened, and Dina slipped quietly into the dock.

Her eyes anxiously searched the courtroom until they found Nick. She smiled wanly in his direction. Nick noticed that she was still wearing the clothes she had on when she left his apartment two days previously. His mind was jerked back to the present when the court reporter called out Dina's name. She rose and stepped in front of the bench. A translator moved to her side, and the young Chinese prosecutor moved to the front and read the charges.

Up to then Nick had not clearly understood what offense Dina had supposedly committed, until he heard prosecutor read them out from the charge sheet in a flat, bored tone . . . "violation of terms of entry . . . illegal hawking . . ." He called an undercover police officer, who took the stand and related how he had observed "the subject" for more than one hour in

Victoria Park and how she had sold magazines and, he thought, been changing money. Nobody challenged his story. The prosecutor then introduced a copy of her employment contract as a domestic helper and sat down.

The judge turned toward Dina and asked if she had anything to say for herself. Nick could barely hear her comments as she slowly answered the judge in English. He gathered that she was trying to explain how she had come to Hong Kong to work ten years ago, and had to earn a living. She sold only harmless things like magazines and phonecards, which she paid for. The judge listened and spoke, not unkindly, "I appreciate your situation, but we have to uphold our immigration laws." Then he sentenced her to two months in jail, suspended. Dina moved back through the side door out of the courtroom.

Nick emerged from the courtroom feeling depressed, and happy, and worried. What did the sentence mean? Would she be released? He flipped open his mobile phone and called Nurma, explained what the judge had said. She seemed optimistic, but cautious. "Did she get a fine?" she asked.

"No." Nick replied. I didn't hear anything about a fine, just a suspended sentence. That's good, right?"

"Yes. That's good," Nurma replied a little skeptically. "What are you going to do now?"

"I'll wait here and see if she is released," he said. Then he hung up.

Nick sat down and waited. He called the fitness center and told them he wouldn't be in that day. Every so often he looked up as a woman exited the courtroom, hoping it was Dina. He looked at his watch. It was already early afternoon. Finally he saw the prosecutor coming out of the courtroom for a smoking break. He went over to him and inquired about Dina.

"Dina . . . he thumbed through his folder . . . I think she's over at Immigration."

"Immigration?" Nick asked. "I thought she got a suspended sentence."

"Yes, she did, but I think Immigration is re-evaluating her status . . . look, I got to go." He put out his cigarette and walked briskly back into the courtroom.

Nick didn't know what to do. The man had said "Immigration," but he didn't know exactly what that meant. He called Nurma back and told her what had happened. She thought for a while and said she'd make some calls and get back to him,. Nick sat back in the bench and waited.

In a few more minutes, his phone buzzed. Nurma was back on the line.

"They've taken her back to Victoria Prison."

"What does that mean?"

"I'm not sure. I think they're reviewing her status."

"I'll go there now."

"I don't think they're letting anyone see her today. Go back to her place and get some clothes together for her. You can see her tomorrow. I'll go with you, if you want."

The next morning, Nick went to Dina's place. The small room seemed strangely quiet and empty without Dina's presence. He looked slowly around the room. Her sofa bed was neatly made, with blankets folded at one end and yellow pillows on top. On top of the television set, was the birthday card he had given her more than a month ago. He opened the dresser and began to rummage though the clothes, wondering which ones to pack. He pulled out a small suitcase and began to fill it. He chose some pants and some shirts, and put in a pair of shoes. At the back of the dresser he found a plastic bag stuffed with rupiah notes. He hesitated whether to put them in the suitcase. They might be stolen in the jail. When he had filled the suitcase, he looked around the room again. His eyes fell on the birthday card, and he picked it up and placed it carefully on top of the clothes. Then he shut the suitcase.

On Paterson Street he caught a taxi to Central, disembarking again on Hollywood Road. He trudged up Old Bailey Street, dragging the suitcase behind him. It was the first time he had gone to Victoria Prison by himself. He found the side entrance, went through the formalities and entered the visitor's room, giving Dina's name to the female corrections officer behind the desk. She took the suitcase and told him to take a seat and wait.

Nick settled down on one of the plastic chairs. Every now and then an officer opened the door to an adjacent room and summoned a visitor inside. He looked at the clock; twenty minutes had passed. He reflected that he had never before visited anyone in jail. He looked around the waiting room, about half full of people, mostly Chinese. He saw no other Westerners. He read the rules posted on the wall, a list of items visitors could not bring to inmates: Shaving cream, snacks, razor blades. Suddenly he heard his name called.

He followed the officer into the next room and sat down in one of the cubicles. Dina was sitting on the other side of the clear plastic partition. For a moment the two just stared at each other. Dina looked tired, and her eyes were red from crying.

"I brought your suitcase," Nick said.

"Thank you," Dina replied. They were silent again.

Finally, Nick said, "Do you know what's going to happen to you?"

"They said they'll fly me back to Indonesia tomorrow morning."

"What?" Nick exclaimed. "Can't you do something? Maybe we can get a lawyer."

"I think it is too late," she replied. "Can you send my other things back home for me? I'll give you my address."

Nick fumbled in his pocket for a pencil and paper. He wrote the address down, as Dina told it to him.

They sat a little longer in silence. Dina pressed her hand against the clear plastic, and Nick put his hand there too. Then the guard came in and tapped Dina on the shoulder. She rose and walked away, still looking back at Nick.

Soon after he exited the prison, he called Nurma and told her what had happened.

"Isn't there anything we can do? Can I at least see her off?"

"No. I think they take them to a holding room before boarding the plane."

"So I can't see her again."

"Don't be sad. Maybe she can find a way to get back. And anyway, you can go to Indonesia."

Nick took the subway back to Causeway Bay. He entered Victoria Park near the new fountain. It was afternoon, and Chinese people were sitting on the benches, feeding the pigeons. The bench where Dina sat every day, selling her magazines and phonecards, was empty. In the distance he heard Chinese boys playing soccer on the concrete pitch next to the big bronze statue of Queen Victoria – looking placidly towards the mountains. He stopped and looked back at the empty bench for a long moment. Then he strode heavily across the broad lawn, back to his apartment.

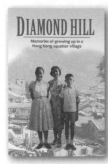

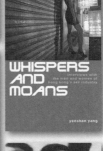
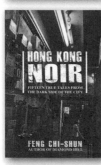